[handwritten inscription]

MW00966769

[handwritten signature] Horner
2/27/16

WHO WILL WATER THE FLOWERS?

Louis Horner

BY

CADET #271
(Louis F. Horner)

© 2016 Cadet 271 AKA Louis Horner

All Rights Reserved.

No part of this publication may be reproduced, stored in a retrieval system, or trans-
mitted, in any form or by any means, electronic, mechanical, photocopying, record-
ing, or otherwise, without the written permission of the author.

First published by Dog Ear Publishing
4011 Vincennes Rd
Indianapolis, IN 46268
www.dogearpublishing.net

ISBN: 978-1-4575-4505-4

This book is printed on acid-free paper.

This book is both autobiographic and historical fiction. Some of the names and actual
events are real.

Printed in the United States of America

INTROSPECTIONS

*M*y classmate, John Nothwang, and I offer these observations that may provoke your thinking in directions you had not previously considered as you navigate through life's journey:

"What we see with our eyes can sometimes cloud our vision, but what we feel in our hearts can never be compromised until the final beat of the drummer of one's heart."

"Use what you've learned from the past to make you believe in the present. Take your beliefs from the present to validate your direction and visions for the future."

"Any journey will have a beginning and an ending; what's important is which path you travel."

"We should focus on valuing sameness not differences.."

"We all cast the same color shadow, but to what extent can your individual shadow be seen and felt by others in your family, workplace, country, and, in some cases, throughout the world?"

"It can be said that we all believed in each other before we believed in ourselves."

"Through our four years together we gave up part of our individuality. In doing so, we developed a set of common goals, ideals, and values."

"While as young men we did not fully realize it, the threads of friendship and respect began to be woven into a fabric for life."

"We believe that our brothers who can no longer hear the bugles have been called to a higher battleground to watch over us as we continue to march on."

"Friendships have sustained themselves over a span of lifetimes." John Nothwang

"We believe we all share pride in the journey, a penchant for honesty, integrity, and grit, and looking back, we realized who we were, who led us there, and in the foundry of cadet life, we were shaped to live our lives of purpose." John Nothwang

To:

the Class of 1957, Stratford High School,
Stratford, Connecticut

the Class of 1958, Peekskill Military Academy,
Peekskill, New York

the Class of 1962, Pennsylvania Military College,
Chester, Pennsylvania

Tuskegee Airmen,
332nd Fighter Group and 477th Bombardment Group,
United States Army Air Corps

#42
Jackie Robinson, Brooklyn Dodgers,
Brooklyn, New York

PREFACE

*T*he content of this book is comprised of historical facts (some edited for literary effect), interviews with classmates, and autobiographical elements. I have chosen to include fictional representations of people, places and events to connect actual facts. The inspiration came from a dream that I felt was a spiritual intervention.

The authentic life stories from my friends and classmates came in response to my survey questions. I compiled this information and presented it in a narrative form to add richness. In some cases, I have used cadet numbers to indentify individuals while protecting their anonymity.

I hope that in your reading, you will realize that this book is not just a story of military college men or corporate executives. I hope that you will see that these stories in some way mirror your own life and that each life story conveys a learning experience.

For many years, this country has talked about and promoted the notion of valuing differences. First, let us talk about valuing sameness. By doing this, we emphasize the factual reality of our sameness and can then utilize this to address the notion of differences.

CONTENTS

PART ONE

LESSONS FROM GEESE

When you see geese flying in a V formation
You might consider what science has discovered
As to why they fly that way.

As each bird flaps its wings, it creates an
uplift for the bird immediately following.

By flying in a V formation, the whole flock
adds at least 71 percent greater flying range
than if each bird flew on its own.

People who share a common direction and sense of
community can get to where they are going more quickly
and easily because they are traveling
on the thrust of one another.

When a goose falls out of formation,
it suddenly feels the drag and resistance of trying
to go it alone and quickly gets back
into formation to take advantage of the
lifting power of the bird in front.

If we have as much sense as geese, we will stay in
formation with those who are headed in
the same direction we are.

When the head goose gets tired, it rotates back to
the wing and another goose flies to the point.

It is sensible to take turns doing demanding jobs,
with people or with geese.

Finally, this is important: When a goose
gets sick, or is wounded by gunshots, and falls
out of formation, two other geese fall out with
that goose and follow it down to lend help and protection.

Those two will stay with the fallen goose until it is
able to fly, or until it dies, and only then will
they launch out on their own, or with another formation,
or catch up with their group.

If we have the sense of geese,
we will stand together like that.

by Dr. Robert McNeish, Baltimore , Md.

TIME OF CHANGE

Flock of migrating Canadian geese at sunset

*T*his was the most exciting, memorable, intriguing, introspective, mesmerizing first day of autumn in my life. It was Friday, a little before dusk. I had left work from Maynard, Massachusetts, for my home, which was a long drive down Route 495. Continuing down Route 24 south, I finally arrived on the last leg of my drive to Route 140 south. This hour-and-a-half drive would bring me to my home in New Bedford, Massachusetts, famous for being the whaling capital of the world. It is said that the last whaling ship sailed out of New Bedford in 1938, a year before I was born.

Several airstreams down Route 140 south serve as pathways for the geese making their way south for their annual migration. There is no greater joy than to be driving at dusk or early in the morning and experience the excitement of looking skyward to see several flocks of geese flying in a V formation. The lead goose of each formation has been entrusted with the direction and safety of the entire formation. I was graced with this beauty on this drive.

As soon as my eyes caught the edge of this beautiful formation of geese, I had to pull over to the shoulder of the highway to get out of my car and look to the sky. A rare moment, not seen by all, encompassed my soul. A full formation, teamed together, flew above my head, relying on each other for shared leadership and clear communication. I was filled with awe and wonder when the lead goose tired and dropped back, and I was intrigued with the communications, pecking order, and selection process in action while I watched another goose move into the lead position. Thus began my journey and awakening.

Mother Nature blessed us with her third seasonal change of the year. With the departure of summer, I saw the first recognizable signs that fall had arrived. The air was crisp, fresh, and invigorating. A sweater or a light jacket therefore became part of my everyday wardrobe. The second sign that fall had arrived was that school was now in session, and Friday and Saturday night gatherings took place at the local high school football fields. Many families who were fortunate enough to own second homes along the New England shorelines started preparing those homes for closure until spring.

AWAKENING

*T*wenty years ago, after arriving at my home and lost in awe about my incredible experience, I decided to retire to bed for some well-deserved sleep after a long day at the office. My home, which I loved very much, was a huge Georgian colonial with brick front, ten rooms, and five bathrooms. Previously owned by a sea captain, my home was adorned with a historical plaque.

I was looking forward to enjoying a weekend of rest and relaxation. Little did I know that my sleep would be interrupted by a brief but powerful spiritual and emotional intervention that I could not entirely understand—one that I will carry with me to the end of my life.

I was awakened by a soft voice. I could not distinguish whether it was a male or female, but this was not the focus of my attention. The voice was telling me that I had the responsibility to write this book and must do it. The voice kept repeating the title of the book: *Who will water the flowers? Who will water the flowers?* A vision of the book cover began to appear and take shape. I saw the image of a black shiny cover with the profile of a cadet outlined in silver. Diagonally across the profile of the cadet was a bright yellow flower with a long green stem. Although I found myself half asleep, groggy, and somewhat startled by an unfamiliar a voice in a darkened room, I was totally consumed with capturing and embracing this awakening. Having converted to Catholicism, I felt that either God or the presence of a choir of angels was delivering me a message of responsibility for writing a book—but about who or what or where had not yet been determined.

I got up from my bed, went downstairs to my office, and sat at my desk. I sat there in the darkness in the quiet of the night for what seemed like hours, trying to understand what I had just experienced. I glanced at the clock only to realize it was three a.m. I thought it would be best to capture on paper what I had just experienced, even though I did not understand the intent or message. After doing so, I put the paper in a safe place in my desk for future reflection.

Over the next twenty years, I took the paper with the handwritten note out of my desk and read it many times. Each time I did so, I tried to grasp and ascertain the meaning and message, to understand the responsibility given to me by this spiritual intervention. In October of 2002, I would come to understand the journey I was about to begin, which has brought my words to you.

Let us begin this journey and together gain a greater understanding and appreciation for the phrase *Who will water the flowers?*

THE MESSAGE

*A*ny journey has a beginning and an ending; most important is the path you travel between the two. What has been endured and accomplished can never be disputed. We each cannot embrace or understand our life journey unless we acknowledge its beginning, its challenges and successes.

This story relates the journey of 265 cadets whose future was not for men with little minds. A retiring general, chief of research and development for the United States Army, emphasized to the 265 members of Pennsylvania Military College, the 141st graduating class, in his commencement address on Sunday, June 3, 1962:

> Faith is not fear.
> Courage is not complacency.
> Patriotism is not patronage.
> Sacrifice is not selfishness.

The general continued, pointing out that the future was not for those with little minds, nor for those who were selfish and vainglorious but for the bold and the brave and the magnanimous. The future is for the men who dare, who have vision, imagination, faith, courage, persistence, wisdom, and patience to transfer their dreams into reality. The general ended his commencement address by saying, "We all must guard against the arrogant intellectual who is now convinced that the world has no creator."

These messages were delivered to the Class of 1962, one of the finest ever, one which called itself the Band of Brothers. This class, Pennsylvania Military College President Clarence R. Moll declared, fulfilled one of his fondest dreams: "These men are intensely oriented educationally and at the same time have attained a high level of military excellence within the Corps of Cadets."

Among these 1962 graduates was the highest percentage of young men ever to attend and graduate from professional schools in the history of Pennsylvania Military College. To the president, this was singularly significant, "because Pennsylvania Military College needs no longer to mimic other colleges in its education program, but instead is ready, as these graduates become independent in decision and action. This has only been possible to achieve because everyone who makes up the Pennsylvania Military College family; trustees, faculty, alumni, parents, friends and students directed themselves energetically and unselfishly to this end."

It is my ultimate wish that you, the reader, will come to understand the all-consuming messages which we as humans may internalize and that serve as our life templates. We, the Pennsylvania Military College Class of 1962, through our identification, leadership, bonding, friendships, accomplishments, and respect for each other, have defined ourselves as the Band of Brothers.

It is my desire to acquaint you with the history of Pennsylvania Military College. It is my hope that you will understand the events that took place in these brick-and-mortar buildings that formed the foundation that allowed the Class of 1962 to define itself and achieve the label as the best to graduate from PMC.

Highlights from the college's history can be found in Appendix A

Old Main

Class of 1962

FROM BOYS TO MEN

*I*n fall 1958, each cadet left his family, friends, high school class-mates, and communities to embark upon a journey. This journey provided each of us with as a unique template for special friendship and lasting memories.

We young men formed these friendships and other bonds at the early ages of eighteen and nineteen. Youth, physical fitness, visions, goals, and careers were of the utmost importance to us as we began the journey to structure our lives. Although as young men we did not fully realize it, the thread of friendship and respect had begun to be woven into the fabric of our lives. We soon learned that Pennsylvania Military College was where we needed to be, and we became known as the Band of Brothers.

Over the next four years, we chose to give up part of our individuality. In doing so, we developed a set of common goals, ideals, and values. We formed strong bonds while marching to the same drummer.

It can be said that at any point in time, each of us can push the pause button on a friendship and later hit start to begin the friendship again. Having not attended the reunions for over forty years, once I did attend it became apparent to me that the bonds remained strong and unique.

The Class of 1962 will always be important to me, as each member of the class is my brother. Each one of my brothers offers a unique friendship. We have, on many occasions, offered thanks to one another for friendship, respect, camaraderie, and the privilege to be members of the Band of Brothers.

We entered our freshman year in September 1958. Pennsylvania Military College had, since its inception 137 years prior, built a tradition of producing leaders. Through a firmly integrated program of academic and military training, the Pennsylvania Military College cadet is prepared emotionally, intellectually, militarily, and spiritually to assume a place of responsibility and leadership in a democratic society. Mindful of this goal, the Pennsylvania Military College stresses an atmosphere of education, offering courses in the arts, sciences, business administration, and engineering.

We came to Pennsylvania Military College with, first, middle, and last names. Somehow, our birth names were quickly replaced with cadet numbers and recognizable nicknames that would last until graduation.

NICKNAMES OF THE BAND OF BROTHERS

Robert Adelman	Adels
John Alexander	Alex
Arnold Barnabei	Darby
George Bennett	Teddy
Marlin Berry	Mar
Ken Blanchard	Doc
Bob Burton	Burt
Wrigg Calvert	Lord Calvert
Barry Case	Midget
Michael Cefalo	Cef
John Conforti	Cables
Walter Crate	Duke
Joseph Deal	Bull
Vincent DeBenedetto	D
William Diament	Pal
Louis DiCave	Lou
Joseph DiEduardo	D
John Dinardo	D
John Dougherty	Doc
Sebastian Faro	Seb
George Fatsy	Fats
Roland Gabriel	Gabe
Jacque Gerard	Cosmo
Richard Gilmore	Gil
Chester Greco	Chet

Karl Groff	Cork
Jon Gruber	Grubs
Bruce Hanley	Crash
Robert Hawley	Hefty
Jack Homan	Jack
George Horn	Hook
Louis Horner	Ring-a-ling
Ronald Houseknect	Zeke
Jerry Jalosky	Jer
Richard Johnson	Ox
Barry Kalinsky	Fatty
Chris Kassimus	Jug
Jack Kehoe	Black Jack
Barry Keith	Bullett
William Kester	You People
Frank Kovach	Ernie
Lawrence Krumanocker	Krum
Peter Lake	Level
Peter Larkin	Lark
James Loftus	Jimbo
Daniel Madish	D-True
Eugene Madzelan	Rail
Thomas McGrath	Quick Draw
John McMahon	Jack
Lawrence Mills	Larry
Adrian Moino	Andy
John Nothwang	Tiger
Rexford Neuman	Alfred E.
Angus Nichols	Nick
Ibrahim Obaid	Bemo
Gary Piff	Piffer
Stewart Portas	Bud
Kenneth Rebert	Reb
Frank Rideout	Sarge
Steven Rising	Blade
Nathaniel Rogers	Buck
Ernesto Sanchez	Tito

Robert Sanders	Bub
Donald Schottland	Shots
Winfred Schubert	Udo
George Shaffer	Shaf
Robert Shore	Moff
George Siekielski	Ace
William Simpson	Will
Joseph Spadafina	Huff
Maury Spang	Doink
Fred Spotts	Ferd
John Tysall	Moose
David Ungerer	Steven Allen
Angel Vega	Pichi
Glen Winn	Gyrene
Donald Zero	Guy
Kurt Zetzshe	Bruhn

The Corps

THE CORPS

*I*n September of each year, thousands of young Americans attend the country's many colleges and universities. They throw great energy and enthusiasm into their work and undertake the difficult task of acquiring the knowledge necessary to make a worthwhile contribution to society. There are, however, a few men who take on an even more difficult task. These young adults not only prepare themselves for civilian life but also acquire the knowledge and skills necessary to protect America from those who would destroy our way of life. The Corps of Cadets of Pennsylvania Military College was comprised of such adults, all male.

What does it mean to a cadet to train for this dual purpose? It is in some measure a sacrifice, for it means giving up freedom of activity and a less disciplined lifestyle associated with civilian college life. It means long hours of study and of practical military exercises. Because the Corps governs itself, cadets placed in positions of responsibility are constantly faced with the need to make decisions. There are but a few easy decisions. Command in itself is not easy and cadets must learn how to command.

A cadet's weekend does not begin on Friday afternoon as it usually does in a civilian school. Saturday mornings are filled with inspections and parades. Thus, Friday evenings must be spent in preparation. In civilian schools, such activities as dances, movies, or fraternity parties seem to be the norm. For a sizable part of the Corps, Saturday and Sunday afternoons may mean guard duty. For the rest, it means a chance for a little rest and relaxation.

The sharpness and precision of the Corps has created a tremendous demand for its presence at ceremonies and parades throughout the country. This means the loss of even more free time, and quite often, the loss of parts of an anticipated furlough. Few who see the smartness and the precision of the Corps's appearance realize the countless number of hours of drill behind it. Few realize the tedious tasks that are necessary to keep the uniforms and equipment perpetually immaculate and polished.

The strenuous mental and physical taxation on the cadets tends to thin out the ranks of the Corps as the year progresses. For some, the strain is just too much. Many, however, are able to meet the challenge and in the end stand up to be counted as some of America's finest young men. I feel it is a distinct honor to capture their stories and proudly give tribute to all. Finally, above all, I am proud to be part of this inspiring story of those cadets who make up the Corps of Cadets.

THE ROOK

*T*he month of November is always highlighted with a special morning event. On one such occasion the sky was filled with ominous clouds indicating that snow or rain was in the forecast, but the change in weather did not dampen the spirits of the fourth-class men. This was our day, as it had been for our predecessors. We had been waiting for this day since the stiff-backed, razor-sharp upperclassmen had first roared, "Mister." Now a year later, we stood straight in front of our cadet companies. No longer were our uniforms ill-fitting; no longer did our faces look blank and confused. Instead, our uniforms were neat, properly fitted, our shoes polished to a glisten, and our stance straight and erect. Our faces, having lost their babyish looks, now reflected our pride and maturity.

It was Rook Day 1959. A new class was about to be received into the Corps. We, the Class of 1962, were now officially part of the men in gray who marched beneath the dome of Pennsylvania Military College.

We, the Class of 1962, now smaller in number, felt empowered to continue our own journey. When the Class of 1959 accepted us into the Corps on that November morning, we felt at ease. The Class of 1962 had cleared the first hurdle and had proven itself worthy of future command.

PMC Parade Dress, 2nd from left, Louis Horner

CAMPUS LIFE

*A*ll young men at the college, with the exception of nearby day students who resided at home, are part of the Pennsylvania Military College Corps of Cadets. Beginning as a private (rook), the cadet may advance in rank until, as an upperclassman and officer, he takes a position of command. In the classroom and in all phases of his cadet life, he is taught the principles of leadership and honor. Upon graduation, he is eligible to earn a commission as a second lieutenant in the US Army Reserve Corps or in the regular Army. Military instruction is considerably enhanced by a six-week period at summer camp between the junior and senior years. Fort Meade, Maryland, and Indian Town Gap are usually cadets' summer home away from home.

A broad athletic program gives every Pennsylvania Military College cadet an opportunity to participate in some sport. As a member of Middle Atlantic States Athletic Conference, Pennsylvania Military College competes with nearby colleges and universities in football, baseball, basketball, track, swimming, wrestling, cross-country, tennis, and rifle. In addition, an excellent intramural program fosters a competitive spirit among the different cadet companies on campus.

Life at Pennsylvania Military College is not all work. A well-rounded calendar of social and cultural events is planned throughout the year. Entertainment consists of lectures, instrumental groups, singers, and movies, all of which are chosen by a committee of student leaders. Probably the most popular social events for the Class of 1962 were the Pennsylvania Military College "hops." These formal affairs were especially noted for their beautiful decorations; traditional among these were the Junior Ring Dance and the Copper Beach Ball. A couple of memorable events were a requested appearance of Maynard Ferguson's Jazz Band and a visit from the Danish gymnastics team.

Two presidents of Pennsylvania Military College shake hands at last year's graduation.

MAJ. GEN. E. E. MacMORELAND, U.S.A. (Ret.)   DR. CLARENCE R. MOLL
President Emeritus   President

DRUM MAJOR

A drum major is a man who leads a marching band or a drum corps, keeping time with a baton. I have chosen the phrase drum major to represent the president of Pennsylvania Military College. His roles and responsibilities over the four years that I participated in the graduation ceremonies always reinforced the importance of his message. As a rook hearing his graduation speech for the first time, I listened with intent. Little did I know that after listening to these graduation speeches, I would internalize the importance of what was being conveyed.

Each year, the words were different, but in the end, the outcome and effect were the same: I once again accepted my moral, social, military, familial, and professional responsibilities as a member of the Corps of Cadets and a citizen of the greatest country in the world, the United States of America. I will feel obligated to do my duty as best I can until the day I die.

I have taken the liberty of analyzing the four presidential graduation speeches that I heard and have put together a compilation of the common themes, values, visions, and responsibilities outlined in them. I came to the conclusion that a common template had been used by the two different drum majors.

Here is the compilation of what I believe were the common themes and messages from the two different drum majors.

Presidential Address

After four years of educational and military studies, you are about to inherit a legacy of tradition, honor, and responsibility. Four years have quickly passed, and you are poised to move forth from these protective walls, a new generation with knowledge of your responsibilities, eager to serve, ready to take the world into your hands, giving it leadership and direction, consciously avoiding the mistakes of your forbears.

In a democratic society, each man is given the opportunity to further his formal and self-education to the full extent of his abilities and ambitions. The extension of a formal education is a privilege, not a right. You have been so privileged.

These things that we have taught you are things we have encouraged you to do. Decisions and judgments require knowledge of the background, understanding of the problem, and some concept of the future. These may only be gained through teaching, learning, and training. All of these things, you have conquered at Pennsylvania Military College. You are truly among the privileged. We are among the privileged who have also been a part of Pennsylvania Military College during its period of most rapid development, to share in its struggle for growth as well as its vision for the future.

Lastly, the degree that each of you has earned represents more than an accumulation of credits or a concentration in subject matter. It represents a spirit and attitude with the ability to analyze and solve problems. This degree represents a cherishing of the ideal as well as the strength of character and moral-well being that are characteristics of the men of Pennsylvania Military College. With this diploma, you accept—and cannot avoid—the responsibility: to perpetuate and elevate the standards on which these precepts of character, leadership, and noble purpose have been developed. The extent to which these things can be achieved depends to a large extent on your success in your chosen professions.

As we leave this chapter, I leave you, the reader, with a question. We all cast the same color shadow, but to what extent can your individual shadow be seen and felt by others in your family, workplace, and country, and throughout the world?

YEARBOOK

*A*s a tribute to and remembrance of four years of educational and military accomplishments, a yearbook, *Saber and Sash,* was completed and distributed, dedicated to the men of the Class of 1962. Each of us initially flipped through the pages in search of his own picture to satisfy his own vanity. Once I had accomplished this mission, I started at the front cover and carefully read through the President's Message, the dedication, the memorial section, and the sections about the educational staff, the senior class, the underclassmen, campus activities, social life, military organizations, and clubs and sports. Having completed this, I found it important to take time to read the individual bios of my classmates and to relive countless memories, experiences, events, and friendships. In many cases, these friendships have sustained themselves over the span of my life. I came to realize something that is most important to me: It can be said that we all believed in each other before we believed in ourselves.

The ritual of the yearbook reading gets repeated time after time again, particularly before a class reunion. This ritual is not specific to Pennsylvania Military College but to all colleges and universities all over the world. Many of the men of the Class of 1962 bring their yearbooks to assist them in recognizing classmates they have not seen in the ensuing years. Painfully but predictably, we learn through discussions that one or more have crossed the bar—been called home by God. In 2004, it occurred to me that some small tribute was needed to acknowledge the fallen men of the Class of 1962.

I had in my possession a list of my brothers who had crossed the bar. I drove to the nearest office-products store and scanned the rows of stickers hanging on the wall. At last, I found what I considered to be the most appropriate small tribute: the American flag. I searched my classmates' yearbook bios one by one, placing an American flag sticker next to the bio of each classmate who had crossed the bar. Then I raised my hand in a taut salute, my little way of saying that we will one day meet again and march together.

Hanging heavily upon me was the revelation that, in time, one of my brothers might read my bio and place an American flag sticker next to my photo, then raise his hand in a taut salute to acknowledge my being called home by God.

As each of us is laid to rest with full military honors, the American flag sticker only symbolizes the true flag that is neatly folded and presented to our loved ones. It is my desire that the tribute will continue beyond me, until every man of the Class of 1962 has an American flag next to his photo, the tribute completed with a taut salute. I also hope the tribute does not just end here. It would be a fitting tribute to plant a bed of red, white, and blue flowers at the base of each headstone marker. The flowers should be perennials to serve as a symbol of continual existence of memories and life. As I completed this symbolic gesture I found it appropriate to ask myself, as I hope each one of you will ask yourself, *Who will water the flowers?* God bless the men of the Class of 1962, the Band of Brothers.

MY FIRST REUNION

*W*hen the word "reunion" is mentioned to most people, it may bring to mind a gathering of family, a high school class, a college class, a rock band, or any other number of groups who decided to gather after a period of separation. When the word "reunion" is spoken to the men of Pennsylvania Military College Class of 1962, it takes on only one connotation: the gathering of the Band of Brothers.

The date was October 12, 2002. The Class of 1962 was gathering at the Marriott Hotel at Philadelphia International Airport for its fortieth reunion. The plan also included homecoming activities on the campus of Widener University, formerly known as Pennsylvania Military College.

Each reunion and homecoming has its unique and special memories. This fortieth reunion was especially important to me. Without any presupposition or knowledge, I was about to be affected for the rest of my life.

It is important that I point out that, for some inexplicable reason, I had not attended a class reunion in forty years. I walked into the reunion reception room and immediately conjured up unfamiliar feelings: warmth of heart, tears, and a sense of guilt. As I looked around the room, my tears were reflections of not only my own feelings but also, in fact, of the tears in some of my brothers' eyes.

What struck me most after processing some of my feelings was how irresponsible and selfish I had been over forty years. I was blinded by the fact that I had allowed the thread of fabric that binds these men to me to fray and stretch for forty years. My absence had nothing to do with my not wanting to be with my brothers; I had been caught up, as many men are, with raising my family and building a career. I had thought I had no right to take time away from my responsibilities to please myself.

Seeing this group of men was like looking into the future. I was now among a different, but somehow the same, college of men: forty years older, some still trim, some heavy, some with full heads of hair, many with receding hairlines, and some who could not see their shoes. What pulled at my heart most that night was the thought of those members of the Class of 1962 who could no longer hear the bugles and march to the drummer. They had been called to a higher battleground to watch over us as we continue through life's march. I could not be more attentive to my brothers, shaking hands with warmth and strength, embracing with true feelings, and letting my smile light the room.

The evening continued with the reaffirmation of friendships, recounts of family and personal experiences, and plenty of toasts to PMC and each other. For those who attended numerous prior reunions, quick updates are all that were needed. Several of my brothers reminisced about our college days and shared stories from their life since college.

When we retreated to our rooms, I knew the weekend was going to give continued meaning to the phrase Band of Brothers. I also realized I had a whole new extended family to love and respect. I would experience homecoming for the first time the following day. I would participate in the traditional march on the field, carrying brooms and the flag standard of the Class of 1962. With all the reconnecting with my brothers, my thoughts were dominated by memories of my awakening of twenty years before and my possession of that little handwritten note. Would God provide me with the long-awaited answer this weekend?

Saturday afternoon at the football game, I marched on the field at halftime for the first time in forty years. I looked at all my brothers marching taut and straight. Looking ahead, I said to myself, "One day some twenty, thirty, or forty years from now, only one of us will be marching on this field representing the Class of 1962." Suddenly, my epiphany took place: I had been chosen to write a book about the Class of 1962. The spiritual energy of the gathering of the Band of Brothers had brought the answer to light.

TWIN TOWERS

Offered by Cadet #363, Class President

Our senior year was to be a culmination of a building process, smooth sailing toward graduation. The traditional One Hundred Days banquet was a real success. The class president learned he had the required credits to graduate and received his acceptance to West Virginia Law School, and another fellow classmate would be with him there. A contingent of the Class of 1962, now took the phrase "building process" a little too literally.

The class president got a visit in his third-floor Turrell Hall room from an upperclassman who wanted to know what was going on. He asked the class president inquisitively, "What are the seniors building in front of Old Main?" The class president sprinted over to the room of two of his fellow seniors to get a view. Sure enough, senior cadets were unloading railroad ties off a commandeered truck. Methodically, twin towers were being constructed, one on each side of the street. A banner emblazoned with the words WELCOME PARENTS TEACHERS ASSOCIATION was finally strung on a rope and tied to the two towers.

Celebrated annually, Parents Day was packed with events. At the end of the day, proud parents and cadets went off campus to dinner, and if the cadet had the required 3.0 GPA, he had earned the privilege to take a weekend leave.

Looking forward to this event, the two dozen or so senior cadets had planned and built the substation edifice dubbed the Twin Towers. All other upperclassmen were rebuffed, and the never-to-be-named seniors did it on their own. The railroad ties had arrived at the far end of the athletic field only a week earlier. The idea had taken form, had been shared among a small group, and had become an irresistible temptation. Our class president observed the construction, chuckled to himself, and anticipated the summons.

Clarence R. Moll, Pennsylvania Military College President, and Colonel Bennett, Commandant of Cadets, jointly summoned the class president to appear in the president's office. President Moll began, "Son, I need you to tell me the names of those cadets involved in last night's incident."

The class president hesitated.

Impatiently, Colonel Bennett jumped in. "Cadet 363, we need the names of those cadets."

The class president felt inspired. "The whole Class of 1962 is responsible, sirs."

All senior officers then got a summons. The order to remove the twin towers was refused. President Moll felt a migraine coming on. Colonel Bennett expressed outrage.

On Friday at 1800 hours, the campus was turned over to the seniors for weekend management. In essence, this meant we ran the office and conducted guard duty. Word spread among our class that the class president's response had been inspirational. We expected all hell to break loose at an anticipated Saturday-morning meeting in the auditorium.

Colonel Bennett, Commandant of Cadets, appeared and ordered all seniors restricted to campus because of a breach of military discipline. President Moll stood nearby and suggested that all senior cadets apologize to their parents and report to their dorms by 0900 hours.

Sunday night, clandestine meetings were held throughout the senior dorms. The grapevine told the story. All agreed that no names were to be revealed. We were all responsible. God bless the Band of Brothers. While restricted to campus, we nevertheless managed to agree on our next course of action. Our hunger strike began at first mess Monday morning.

First mess came around, along with the *Philadelphia Enquirer* and local television reporters and cameras. New York papers called Pennsylvania Military College, seeking commentary. Again, the class president was called to the president's office. In a conciliatory tone, President Clarence R. Moll asked for the names of the senior cadets who had built the Twin Towers. He added that only those directly responsible should pay the price for their actions. The class president stood firm in the knowledge that he had the support of the Band of Brothers.

The Cadet Senior Class was informed that there would be no graduation, no military commissions, and no Class of 1962 for Pennsylvania Military College.

No food was eaten at second mess by the senior class, and by then, the junior class supported our efforts. The grapevine told us that by third mess, the cadet sophomores and freshmen would also join our hunger strike.

Clarence R. Moll, President, ordered the Class of 1962 to the auditorium. President Moll began by saying, "Gentlemen, the hunger strike must end. Only those responsible for the construction of the Twin Towers should face the penalties required for this misdeed. As honorable men, I ask those individuals to take responsibility."

We were left alone for ten minutes to discuss the situation. We agreed on a united front and would stand firm. God bless the Band of Brothers.

Colonel Bennett stepped forward. In a firm military voice, he said, "Will those responsible for this misdeed now stand up?"

In unison, we said, "Yes, sir."

Smiles of relief were evident on faces of the commandant of cadets and the president.

A soft shuffling of feet was heard in an otherwise silent auditorium. Ten cadet seniors stood at attention. As time passed—it felt like a lifetime—fifteen more cadet seniors stood to attention. A short time later, five more cadet seniors stood to attention. Just as we had planned, this united declaration continued for well past one hour. When all 265 senior cadets were standing at attention, we declared in unison, "We, the Class of 1962, are responsible for this misdeed. God bless the Band of Brothers."

We continued to be restricted to campus. The kitchen staff was obligated to prepare food. Because food was being wasted and jobs were possibly being jeopardized, the Class of 1962 agreed to end the hunger strike.

Once again, the class president was summoned to the president's office. President Clarence R. Moll suggested to the class president that if the Class of 1962 were to write a letter of apology to Pennsylvania Military College, the apology would likely be accepted.

The letter of apology was authored by the cadet senior class. The Class of 1962 assured the college that our future actions would be in accordance with acceptable standards for cadet senior classmen.

President Clarence R. Moll then sent a letter to all parents of the Class of 1962. Graduation, the awarding of diplomas, and the awarding of military commissions as second lieutenants would occur as previously scheduled. The cadet seniors felt like they heard a collective, country-wide, parental sigh.

We did not know then but learned later that President Moll had wanted to end the situation early on. He had actually admired our unity and bond. The act, sometimes called a misdeed, was a college prank. We did not lie, and no one was hurt. On graduation day, we walked a little more erect and felt like a true band of brothers.

THE MOVIE THEATER

Offered by Cadet #271

*M*ost college students spent the summer before their senior year working summer jobs, hanging out at the beach, drinking cases of beer, and trying to develop a summer love (if you know what I mean), with a soundtrack of their favorite rock 'n' roll or rhythm and blues.

The phrase "summer love" took on a whole different connotation for the Band of Brothers. It wasn't the beach, but oh God, it was sandy. There were no seagulls to be found, but oh God, the mosquitoes found us in the infested wilderness. There was no "summer love" on a blanket on a moonlit beach but in a hastily dug foxhole as we shared water out of a canteen and Meals, Ready-to-Eat out of cans. This was where the Band of Brothers spent its summer before senior year. Do you know anyone who would consider taking a summer vacation at Indian Town Gap in Pennsylvania or Fort Meade in Maryland? Well, guess what? That's where we spent our summer.

We learned a whole new set of phrases and vocabulary: up and at 'em, SOS, lock and load, Maggie's drawers, check our socks, say ah, bend over, turn your head and cough, your helmet is your pillow, be tactical, hurry up and wait, down in the pits, and slide up and slide down. Our "summer love" was our love for each other. Little did we know that this love for each other would get tested on our weekend trip to Baltimore, Maryland, in 1961.

A contingent of fifteen cadet seniors decided that they were going to take in a movie during their weekend trek to Baltimore. There I was, the only slightly tanned cadet, accompanied by my fourteen brothers, who appeared to be several shades lighter in color, perhaps even a little sunburned, entering the front doors of the movie theater.

I, from the North, unknowingly approached the ticket booth first to purchase my ticket for admission. The woman in the ticket booth indicated that my ticket would be for upstairs in the black section of the theater. As she looked past me at my lighter-skinned brothers, she asked me if I still wanted to purchase a ticket. Having grown up in the North, and not having visited the South before, I was taken aback by her question.

Before I could recover from my shock and embarrassment, I heard one of my brothers shout, "*Bullshit!* We want to purchase fourteen more tickets for admission for upstairs in the black section." He continued, "If this is a problem, I think a bigger problem is about to occur." To this day, I don't even remember what the movie was, but I do remember all of the black people sitting upstairs staring at us, whispering and wondering what all these whiter shades of pale were doing, sitting up there with a not-so-pale brother. Some forty years later, this demonstration of loyalty still cements the love, respect, and humility that I feel for my Band of Brothers. On that day, integration was spontaneous. Amen.

THE LAUNDROMAT

Offered by the wife of Cadet #245

I was born in Germany but grew up in Zurich, Switzerland. I returned to Heidelberg, Germany, in 1963 and met my future husband, a United States Army Officer stationed in Mannheim, Germany. We were married a year later and within a year found ourselves headed to Fort Polk, Louisiana. This was my first trip to the United States. Fort Polk had only three officers' homes, none intended for a captain. After a few days of apartment hunting, we found a small one-bedroom second-story apartment, about ten miles from Fort Polk. The list of things it did not have was far larger than the features it did have, including a place for a washer and a dryer. It was here that I learned the workings of a laundromat, or at least thought I had.

My first trip to the laundromat in the rural South was an eye-opener. The only facility in town consisted of two buildings side by side. One was clearly labeled "coloreds only" and the other was labeled "whites only."

Now, I understood that laundry should be separated into colored and white loads, but a separate building for each type was a bit much. But since this was my first cultural experience in the United States and especially in the deep South, I dutifully separated my wash and spent the next hour or so running back and forth between the two buildings. The fact that I was the only one doing this did not occur to me, but it certainly drew the stares of other customers in both buildings.

I left worn out and determined somehow to include our own washer and dryer in our own lives. Doing laundry in America was far too complicated. I began to hope that grocery shopping would not involve separate buildings for canned goods, fresh produce, and so on. My college education in Europe never included anything about the clearly complex American lifestyle.

That night, when I relayed this cumbersome laundry procedure to my husband, he simply looked at me in disbelief. I was glad he seemed to share my amazement at having to do your white wash in one building and your colored wash in another building. As you can guess, that is not what amazed him. Rather, he was amazed at my interpretation of the meaning of the signs over the laundromat's doors. When he explained the real intent of the signs, I felt embarrassed, surprised, angry, and sad that it should be this way.

As I write this in 2005, I think how fortunate we are to have only one building.

THE DRIVE-IN THEATER

Offered by Cadet #271

After another week of classroom education, study halls, reveilles, room inspections, formations, parade drills, and more formations, the weekend was finally here. The weekend didn't begin until after formations and room inspections on Saturday morning; if you made it through the five and a half days, you were free for the weekend.

Two other cadets and I were sitting in the dorm, trying to decide what we were going to do this Saturday night. We finally decided we would purchase a couple cases of beer, go get my car, which was not allowed on campus, and go to the drive-in theater to see the movie *The Alamo*, starring John Wayne. We went off campus to do just that.

The movie, with lots of action and historical content, was very popular. The drive-in was pretty well filled by the time we got there. We drove around for some time and finally found a parking spot with a speaker that worked. Our parking spot was in a middle row in the center of the drive-in but was, unfortunately, not too close to the snack bar or restrooms. When you decide to take two cases of beer to the drive-in theater, you should consider parking strategically close to the restrooms. When you do the math on the content of two cases of beer, it translates into forty-eight cans divided between three cadets, or, more specifically, sixteen cans of beer each. We knew to drink it, give it away, or throw it away, because we couldn't bring it back.

Fortunately, or unfortunately, our parking spot in the middle of the drive-in and with a working speaker was next to a carload of women from Swarthmore College. After being confined with our fellow cadets all week, we were locked and loaded for at least some conversation and a few laughs. Did I say a few laughs? Let me share with you that with each can of beer, the laughter increased. We shared our beer with our newfound friends, and the movie probably started, but we didn't care.

After several trips to the restroom, I got what I thought was a bright idea. I decided to employ some mechanical engineering and common sense to reduce my frequent trips to the restroom. In 1962, flip top cans were nonexistent; all beer cans had to be opened with an instrument commonly known as a church key. After finishing what had to be at least my sixth can of beer, I opened the can completely around the edge to gain a wider opening and advantage. By doing this, I could now "drain the lizard" once the beer was empty, open the car door, set the can down outside the car, and keep on talking to the women who were parked directly on my left. I was proud of myself.

Pennsylvania Military College ingenuity worked great at least the first six times. I was not as ingenious as I thought on the seventh try, however. Finally, while talking and laughing with my brothers and the women from Swarthmore College, I erroneously neglected to use the church key to effectively push the triangles of tin back to the outer edge. Surprise, surprise! The "lizard" went into the can and got drained but was not cooperating in terms of an exit strategy. The triangular points of tin were aimed directly at the lizard. I said to myself, "Oh, God, what the hell am I going to do now?" I enjoyed no strategic advantage as I was impeded by the steering wheel of my own car. My brothers were continuing their conversations and laughter with the women in the car next to us. At that point, not only my brothers but also the women wanted to know why I had dropped out of the conversation, was silent, and had a questionable look on my face. At that point, I made only my brothers aware of a very tenuous and at least tender situation. My brother sitting in the front seat looked over and observed my predicament. "Do all you black guys have this problem and need to show off?" he asked. My brother in the backseat took it upon himself to tell the women about my predicament.

It became clear after much anxious laughter that the only way to dislodge the lizard from the can was to open my car door, stand straight up, and perform a strange wiggle dance. The laughter from the ladies was deafening. Unfortunately, since we were parked in the center of the drive-in and I had been standing up outside my car and all this laughter was taking place, I was greeted with headlights and beeping horns. To this day, I have never seen the movie *The Alamo*, nor ever again experienced such embarrassment.

THEIR JOURNEYS, THEIR STORIES

*A*fter attending my first reunion I was struck by the fact that me and my classmates started our own journeys from different socioeconomic environments but, through the grace of God, we all made the same decision to enroll at Pennsylvania Military College.

These thoughts fueled my desire to develop a questionnaire for all of my brothers who would be attending the next reunion. These questions could not be answered with "yes" or "no." The questions, carefully crafted, were meant to provoke introspection and thinking. Some of my classmates stated that the completion of this questionnaire took them as much as five to six hours.

Ultimately, the responses to these questions evolved into narratives of each of the cadets' lives. I feel that each of my brothers read and answered the questions going far beyond just the facts. Through their unique individuality, they reflected their experiences, accomplishments, failures, and relationships. They shared information about successful and unsuccessful business ventures. In their life stories, they wrote about spouses, families, tragedies, and critical moments. Here are their journeys, their stories.

Cadet #23
George Bennett

George Francis Bennett

I went to Pennsylvania Military College because ever since I was a very young man, I wanted to go to West Point. While in high school, I did not know anyone who could politically recommend me and I was not all that comfortable with the physical fitness test, etc. One day, I opened a letter from Pennsylvania Military College. I knew then that PMC was for me. I took the test and was accepted.

I went to Pennsylvania Military College because of the military school environment and believed it would make me a more disciplined person. I believed myself, at the time, to be a highly undisciplined/disciplined person. I really found it difficult with getting into step with needing a shave daily, weekly haircuts, and highly shined shoes.

My belief is that I have acquired a very high internal discipline which has seen me through life and in fact has probably kept me alive in various situations. This I attribute to Pennsylvania Military College. My major problem in life and even now has been my lack of being a political person. I still tend to blunder into situations. Pennsylvania Military College taught me to be a moral person who at least tries to do the right thing. A recent example of this occurred this past Sunday when I met a man about four foot eleven in an Air Force colonel's uniform wearing a combat infantryman's badge with two stars. He said he was in Vietnam and two Gulf wars. He looked a mess and did not satisfy me when I asked him about the CIB with two stars. *Hogwash.* After speaking to him, I called the sheriff's office and had the sheriff question the charitable solicitations of the man in uniform, which I believed to be a scam. My beliefs and my assumptions were correct.

At Pennsylvania Military College, you always knew when "the shit was going to hit the fan" in some fashion. Personal discipline and the union of the Class of 1962 made it all bearable.

You always knew there were no favorites. A good example of this was how I felt about our athletes who were not treated properly. During the first week of our freshman year, I witnessed our star football player getting totally reamed out after a hard football practice. Our athletes had to endure everything everyone else did and more. Another story was of the same football star telling Dr. Nearing that he would have to miss a test because of a football trip. Dr. Nearing said, "It would be better if you took the test before the game rather than after it." So, sure enough, the player did just that. He took the exam a full day ahead of everyone else.

The most significant thing that I can remember is how a group of guys from all over the country could come together. At the time of my admittance to PMC, although born in New Jersey, I was really a country boy from Ohio. I remember seeing the statistics of where everyone was from and that only a couple of men came from Ohio. For me, it was either Ohio State or Pennsylvania Military College. My parents never pushed me. I decided to attend Pennsylvania Military College.

I should point out at this time that from an early age I knew I was sometimes a loose cannon with an extremely low boiling point. Many times words would come into my head and out of my mouth without thought. At Pennsylvania Military College I cannot tell you the number of push-ups I did for speaking too quickly.

I have kept in contact most with Cadet #471. In fact, I stayed at his home during the forty-second reunion. I had run into him from time to time since graduation. The biggest influence was shortly after graduation. Cadet #471 was ahead of me at Fort Benning and Fort Holabird. At Fort Benning, he asked me if I would be in his wedding, and I agreed. Then at Fort Holabird, he reminded me that it seemed like it was the last thing that I wanted to do. At the time, I was hot on the track of several relationships. To make a long story short, I met my future wife at the wedding of Cadet #471. We have been married a little over forty years, and we met because I had given my word and kept it. Recently, I have done some work as an insurance agent at a small hospital owned by Cadet #471 in Mississippi.

The biggest event in my life was really a combination of things which caused the Class of 1962 to be a united group. At a recent reunion, the most salient point was that everyone truly liked each other. I, like others, contemplated transferring. I'm glad I didn't. I would have missed it too much.

It is with much sadness that I share the news that since sharing his story with me, Cadet #23 has crossed the bar.

Cadet #28
Joseph Berarducci

Joseph S. Berarducci

I had two early life ambitions. One was to make the Army my career, and the other was to go to law school. Law school was, at that time, a far-off venture, but West Point was a nearby dream. However, I found out too late from my counselor that the appointment for my district was taken. He recommended attending a military college for one year and then applying again to West Point. I had looked at Norwich University, Virginia Military Institute, and Pennsylvania Military College. Virginia Military Institute and Norwich University seemed far away and rather alien, so I settled on Pennsylvania Military College, which was located in my home state.

Of course, after one year at Pennsylvania Military College, I lost my interest in West Point. I asked myself the question, "Who wants to start all over again?" I pretty much had settled into Pennsylvania Military College, or had as much as one can after one year. I then began to turn my attention more to my academics than I had ever done before. I thought it was a bit wiser to stay the course.

I am not sure I can remember or pinpoint significant events about Pennsylvania Military College. What sticks out most in my mind are those things that I think we all remember, or that any memorable college experience brings to mind. For example, the formation of long-lasting friendships, the dumb if not dangerous adventures we all undertook, etc. I think for me the most significant event that I clearly remember is a transformation that took place.

When asked how did I think I had changed as an individual during my four years at Pennsylvania Military College, I reflected that this is an important question. It brings up the most significant event that I remember about PMC. Like so many other boys, I was a high school kid who had his mind only on sports, girls, and good times. Academics were a sideline. Pennsylvania Military College transformed me into a serious student with a real interest in academics and academic study. I attribute this to the general atmosphere of strict discipline in our daily life—a rather Spartan life—and to a very strict study routine. Where else do you get locked up in your room from seven p.m. to ten fifteen p.m. six nights a week? So the most significant event or change at Pennsylvania Military College was a transformation from a frivolous kid to a serious person.

As I think about four years at Pennsylvania Military College, I had a profound change of ambition with regards to my military career. I drifted away from my initial ambition to make the Army my career. It isn't that Pennsylvania Military College had changed my mind about a military career so much as I had changed and began to migrate towards more serious thoughts of law school. So a military college environment actually caused me to drift away from a military career.

I now began taking more time to think about my future professional life and career outside of the military. In the second semester of my sophomore year, I began planning on law school. With that thought in mind, I considered transferring and began making applications to other colleges. I think the front office at Pennsylvania Military College got wind of this through requests for transcripts from the schools that I had applied to. Because of this, I received a call from the president, Dr. Clarence R. Moll, requesting to meet with me. So in I walk, and he and Colonel Cottee are sitting there. As I recall, they asked me why I wanted to transfer, was I unhappy, what complaints did I have, etc. I was not ready for this particular question, so I said, "Yes, the laundry. My socks come back with lint on them." Dr. Moll looked at me with a straight face and said, "Anything else?" I said, "No, sir, that's about it."

About two weeks later, I received a call from Colonel Cottee's office offering me a small scholarship if I decided to stay. Ironically, I already had a small grant of four hundred dollars, so this additional offer was attractive.

I think it was during the Easter vacation while I was at home on furlough I received the acceptance letter from the University of Pennsylvania. I had already told my parents about the additional offer of a small scholarship at Pennsylvania Military College. My father took one look at the tuition at the University of Pennsylvania and decided that I would be financially better served in continuing my academics at PMC. I can honestly say I never regretted it.

As I now begin to expand my thoughts about pleasant memories and/or experiences, I cannot pinpoint a particular event. However, I always remember the feeling that we at Pennsylvania Military College were different than other college students. They had their fraternities, their parties, etc., but they were not part of the Long Gray Line. That made me feel special, and that, of course, was probably nothing more than an ego thing. What I learned from this is that it's nice to feel special.

The downside of pleasant memories and experiences is your worst memories and experiences. My worst memory was a single event. Two of my fellow classmates and I went on a Sunday-afternoon drinking binge in our sophomore year. We returned for sign-in at seven p.m. As I recall, sign-in was at the adjutant's office in Old Main. The process was you walked in one at a time, saluted, and gave your cadet number, did an about-face, and left the room. The next cadet in line in the hallway took his turn and repeated the process. We noticed Captain D in the room, and I thought we would all have a heart attack. One of my classmates went first, then me. Hoorah, we both made it. Then my other classmate went in and never came out. It was as though he had disappeared into a black hole. We both returned to our rooms in Howell Hall. We never got to see our other classmate, who went last that night. I just waited in agony for my name to come over the loudspeaker ordering me to return to the adjutant's office. The worst thoughts were running through my mind. The announcement never came. When I finally saw my classmate the next day, he told me that Captain D called him into the side office and asked him where he had been drinking and with whom. He admitted to drinking but said it was alone. He stuck to his story and covered our backsides. He marched tours every day until the end of the year. My classmate, my friend, and I often talk about this. We laugh now, but it is still a bad memory.

It can be said that this experience was an act of friendship, although I cannot say that any single friendship made a great impression or had a great impact on my adult life. What has made a great impression or impact is the totality of all of my friendships.

The one single event that has sustained my friendships at Pennsylvania Military College has been the annual reunions. I attend them because they are thoroughly enjoyable. What is so amazing is that we may not see one another for some time, but within five minutes at these reunions it's like we never left Pennsylvania Military College. We pick up where we left off and there is no time gap. It's a continuous flow of love and laughter that never ends. Just as I have enjoyed my friendships during my four years at PMC, I find that I will continue to enjoy them until I cross over the bar.

I now would like to share with each one of you my continuing journey after leaving Pennsylvania Military College. I went to Dickinson Law

School. Law school is not a breeze and is not for the weak of heart. You must be tough and work hard or you will find yourself looking for another line of work. I had a very successful school career. I was third in my class and nominated to the law journal staff (limited to fifteen people). It is the highest academic award in any law school. I published two articles while at Dickinson. I clerked one summer with the government in their honors program. I was selected for the Office of the General Counsel for the Internal Revenue Service, again limited to fifteen people from all law schools nationwide. I attribute that success to the discipline and work ethic I learned at Pennsylvania Military College. For me there could not have been any better preparation.

After law school, I spent three and one half years on active duty. I was in a military intelligence detachment with the Eighth Special Forces Group. I was actually interviewed three times before volunteering for this assignment. It turned out to be a life adventure. The headquarters at the time was in the Canal Zone, but we moved out in teams in Central and South America, doing on-the-job training in guerilla or counterinsurgency warfare. It was some experience, and I learned a lot. Except for a few potshots here and there, I was not in harm's way, but it was not easy and there were a lot of dangerous people around us.

After leaving the Army, I took my first job with a law firm in Harrisburg, Pennsylvania. It turned out to be a miserable time. I was like a fish out of water. It was a stuffy old place that I did not fit into. I took the job because one of my senior partners was a professor at Dickinson Law School and was a favorite of mine. It turned out to be a big disappointment. I left after about two years, shortly after my first marriage.

My next job was with the District Attorney's Office in Philadelphia. I was assigned to the felony trial division and ended my tenure four years later in the major crimes division. I enjoyed my time here and had some success in my work as a prosecutor. The job was a learning experience, and it gave me an opportunity to sharpen my trial skills and develop some new ones. After four years, I left the office and returned to private practice with a small trial firm in Philadelphia.

For the next five years, I did general trial practice. We had a successful small practice and things were going good. Then the two senior partners began to quarrel and slowly but surely, things began to unravel. I had no choice but to leave, and within a year, the firm dissolved.

Things got tough financially. I was married, with two young children and a recently purchased home. I had a tiny client base and a large drop in income. It was a slow struggle up; yes, very slow. Then personal tragedy came upon me. I experienced a divorce and a devastating house fire while I was home. These were followed years later by the unexpected death of my son at age thirty-one. Life was challenging in those years.

But things did get better. I remarried, and my present wife and I have a very nice life and relationship. The practice did get much better, and today I can honestly say things are going well. "All's well that ends well."

And finally, as I think about the threads that bind us, much like "Lessons from Geese," it is often said that people who have shared some difficult or stressful time together such as 9-11, the Depression, combat, etc., are bound together by that common experience. Our years at Pennsylvania Military College do not, of course, rise to that level, but it was a common discipline and cloistered environment, if not Spartan life that few other people have experienced. It is that that binds us together and which we all have in common. Pennsylvania Military College and that era no longer exist, but the threads that bind live in every one of us.

Cadet #224
Bruce Hanley

Bruce Martin Hanley

My thoughts, recollections and memories during and after attending four years at Pennsylvania Military College I would like to share with each one of you. They may not be in any special order. I find I am more factual and emotional when I outline in this manner. So here goes.

My dad passed away in 1956 when I was sixteen. The Korean Conflict had recently ended and my mother wanted me to get a college education, go into the service, and go in as an officer. Military college was the best option. I looked at Norwich University in Vermont and Pennsylvania Military College in Chester, Pennsylvania. After a home visit from Professor Harold Smith, I chose Pennsylvania Military College.

The most significant event that I remember was the Class of 1962 constructing the twin towers on Friday night from railroad ties on Parents' Weekend. One of my fellow senior cadets came back from wherever, "hell-bent for election" in his car and driving on the sidewalk in front of Old Main. It scared the daylights out of us. Our entire class was grounded for the weekend. We were called into the auditorium. (Not all of our classmates participated in the construction of the twin towers.) We were chewed out, reprimanded, and grounded for the weekend by Major Gossett, Captain DeSerafino. We were also asked who was responsible. The Class of 1962 stuck together; no one stepped forward as the perpetrator(s).

Another fond memory was our hundred day's graduation banquet at the Media Inn. We had the owner call campus to the officer of the day, Captain James Culver, advising him that cadets were rowdy and unruly and he should come out and assess the situation. It was a ploy. He was my TAC officer and had just received his orders to Vietnam as an advisor, and we wanted to show our appreciation to him by having him join us before he shipped out. He recognized my leadership abilities on campus and summer camp. He made the greatest impression on me at Pennsylvania Military College.

Another was the "little Army–Navy game," better known as the Boardwalk Bowl, at the Convention Hall in Atlantic City, New Jersey, when we played the United States Merchant Marine Academy. Watching our fullback classmate and junior quarterback take over the field, it can be said we came, we saw, we conquered. The score: thirty-five to fourteen. Also, the entire Corps of Cadets in formation on the boardwalk was a sight to behold.

Passing the Graduate Record Exams and receiving my diploma with a Bachelor of Arts in English was the culmination of determination, focus and four years of attitude adjustment.

Going back and reliving my freshman year, in 1958, I recall that after two weeks on campus as a rook with a cadre on top of you and in your face twenty-four–seven, I wanted out. I called home; however, my mother, who was a very strong individual, convinced me to give it time and stick it out. In retrospect, it was the best thing I ever did. I don't believe a civilian school would have provided the discipline and the character building that Pennsylvania Military College provided. For that opportunity, I am truly grateful. Being in the Corps of Cadets caused me to appreciate the free time of weekends and furloughs more. I was 240 pounds with a forty-one inch waist that August of 1958. My first time home was for Thanksgiving; I was 190 with a thirty-eight inch waist. My mother did not recognize me when I came to the door.

Four years at Pennsylvania Military College taught me flexibility and attitude and how to adjust to the disappointments that life gives you. A major disappointment was not being part of the commissioning ceremonies at graduation. Being designated a distinguished military student and distinguished military graduate, I had planned to make a career of the service. These hopes were dashed due to a high school football injury to my left knee which developed traumatic arthritis. I applied for the Marine Corps PLC program in my junior year and took the physical at Saint Albans Naval Hospital in Long Island, New York. After the physical and x-ray exams, a Marine major doctor came to me and said, "Son, who do you know at the Pentagon?" I said, "No one, sir." He said, "Too bad. You are not eligible for the service." Six weeks before graduation, I tried again. I presented myself at the Philadelphia Quartermaster Depot for the regular Army physical as a distinguished military graduate. Again, no dice.

I was relentless to try and get into the service. I wrote to President John F. Kennedy before his assassination, asking for special consideration, and received letters from the adjutant general and surgeon general declining my request. Needless to say, I had to scurry around for job interviews after this news.

I was subsequently hired by Liberty Mutual Insurance Company as a claims adjuster. I did not like it. I tried the Connecticut State Police and the Los Angeles County Sheriff's Department. Once again, I was disappointed due to traumatic arthritis. After moving to California in

1963, I landed a job with Ford Motor Company; I stayed for ten and a half years. Then I went back to Chicago in 1968 to the Lincoln Mercury Division. Finally after a short stint in self-employment, I worked eight and a half years with Volkswagen of America. Since 1988, I have been self- employed as an insurance agent/broker in Woodstock, Illinois.

My interpersonal relationships with family and friends have been invaluable due to my four years of attendance at Pennsylvania Military College. With the discipline and character building it provided, it allowed me to adjust to life's disappointments and share with my family and friends what it means to be able to move on with your life while sharing faith and giving courage to others. God will provide for those that believe in him.

Through the years I've stayed in touch with my senior-year roommate and my friend, Cadet #339, who was my next-door neighbor in California. I also stayed in touch with another of my classmates, Cadet #383, and, of course, with others at the five-year reunions. However, the Class of 1962 as a whole has special meaning to me. For the past forty-six years, our Class of 1962 has been unique in its esprit de corps, united in taking chances and bearing the consequences, and united in brotherly love extended in times of sorrow.

The outpouring of love and concern for my well-being by my classmates will never be forgotten. My wife passed away on February 16, 2004, from breast cancer, four days short of our thirty-ninth wedding anniversary. Yet two weeks prior, on February 2, 2004, our fifth grandchild was born, whom she was able to hold. I firmly believe she was waiting for that event before the Lord called her home. There is definitely the example of the cycle of life in a family. I have four children and five grandchildren. My life partner was my wife, lover, and friend and had the greatest impact on my adult life.

Reunions are important to me for reflection on my youth and seeing my mates, catching up on earlier days and current events in their lives. When I see them, it's like we are back at Pennsylvania Military College, uniform and all, physical changes—yes, the person as he was, how beautiful, what a reflection. The bonding becomes more important at these reunions due to friendships made between spouses, and each one looking forward to the next. Ill health, and demises of mates and spouses have prompted us, the Class of 1962, to meet more frequently off campus to enjoy those bonding relationships.

And finally, let me share with you my most memorable flashback. I was traveling from Los Angeles to Detroit for a management training seminar with Ford Motor Company in 1963. I flew on to New York after the seminar to see my mother in Connecticut. My return flight was from New York to San Francisco for another seminar. This was a United flight, and this blonde flight attendant walked by and I asked for a glass of milk.

She responded, "What's the matter; do you have an ulcer?"

I said, "Yes."

She provided me with the milk; however, she was not working in my cabin. Later in the flight, I spoke to her in the galley and asked her for another glass of milk, and I asked her out for a drink after the flight.

She gave me the milk and said, "I don't date passengers."

Needless to say, we did go out and we did marry. From the time we met on the plane, we were engaged thirty days later and married in six months.

The Band of Brothers, Class of 1962, is uniquely one. The reunions strengthen that bond. We reconnect. Whether you've been to each one every five years or for the first time at the forty-second reunion, the camaraderie is there and welcomed with brotherly love. The Class of 1962 is one and united forever.

It is with much sadness that I share the news that since sharing his story with me, Cadet #224 has been called home by God.

Cadet #234

Michael Helpa

Bruce Martin Hanley

When I think back as to what prompted me to enroll in Pennsylvania Military College, it made me realize I had never heard of PMC until I received a call from an admissions representative who was in New Jersey, recruiting high school seniors. I scheduled an appointment with the admissions representative at my parents' house, then made a visit to Chester, Pennsylvania, and waited for a financial aid offer. I received a four-year package for a one-half tuition scholarship. My parents were excited about that, and my grandfather was especially pleased that I was accepted into a military college. I liked the fact that a civil engineering curriculum was offered, and with it being a relatively small school, my chances to participate in varsity sports would be competitive.

During my four years of attending Pennsylvania Military College, several significant events took place that I can remember. There was the change in leadership as Dr. Clarence R. Moll was appointed president. There were the beginning of new construction projects, for example, new dorms, never imagining what was to develop both in the near future and long-term future of the college. Other significant events that I remember include the Junior Ring Dance and spending my summer at Fort Meade, Maryland, and at Indian Town Gap, Pennsylvania. The attendance of the Corp of Cadets at the Boardwalk Bowl in Atlantic City, New Jersey was an event to be remembered. Perhaps most significant after attending PMC for four years was receiving a baccalaureate degree and being commissioned as a second lieutenant in the United States Army.

If I were to be asked how I was changed as an individual during my four years at Pennsylvania Military College, I would have to respond in the following manner: The military environment strengthened my beliefs in discipline and organization and taught me how to plan to achieve my goals. I recognize early on that planning options must be considered to meet various situations, and contingencies must be developed to meet the unexpected. Most importantly, teamwork, trust in others, and acceptance of responsibility are essential to achieve common goals. These changes are most definitely different than what would have occurred had I made a decision to attend a nonmilitary college. Also, one of the unique factors at Pennsylvania Military College which contributed to these changes was the structured military environment which minimized external distractions.

After graduating from Pennsylvania Military College, those changes have specific influence on my life in my military career, professional life outside of the military, and consistently in my personal life, including interpersonal relationships with family and friends. An example of what I have conveyed about my professional life was indicated by the civil engineering program that was very small and allowed for much individual attention, resulting in a high quality of learning. The faculty members were interested in each student and very supportive both inside the classroom and out. The quality of education, coupled with the military lifestyle, resulted in a well-rounded background to meet the many challenges of being a part of a workforce.

I recall many pleasant memories and experiences while attending Pennsylvania Military College. Here are just a few that I'd like to share. I participated in varsity baseball for four years, and also, I engaged in intramural sports, football, and basketball. The Junior-Senior Football Classic was one of my fondest memories. It doesn't sound like pleasant memories or experiences, but dress parades and Saturday-morning inspections can be added to this list. The success of these activities was obtained through discipline and teamwork, including the repetitive practices and the assistance to and from others to obtain the desired results.

The downside of attending Pennsylvania Military College for four years is my worst memory. I feel so blessed that the only bad experience I encountered was attending a military dance with a blind date. What I learned from this is that you should always know what you are dealing with before you commit. Good intelligence makes good execution.

I should add at this point that I did not ever contemplate transferring from Pennsylvania Military College to another school.

Having listened to four presidential addresses I can say that the learnings, beliefs, and life messages were internalized in the following way: Success requires dedication, knowledge, discipline, organization, trust, and teamwork while accepting responsibility that comes from one's actions.

I do not believe that I can single out any one individual whose friendship made the single greatest impression upon me while attending Pennsylvania Military College. The overall four-year experience as a class and the outstanding support from faculty members formed a total education process that prepared me to meet life's challenges with a sound foundation.

Looking back at my life, the one single friendship that I had formed that had the greatest impact on my adult life has without a doubt been my marriage to my wife of forty-one years. She has been my lifeline in good times and bad, for family, professional development, social interaction, and individual growth.

The reunions are important to me because they bring the gathering of friends to me face-to-face to relive the good times, share experiences, and provide support as necessary. It is important to me to continue to attend as a way of maintaining those friendships. And finally, the common threads that bind the men of the Class of 1962 is the trust that was formed in us as a class through reaching out to help each other through teamwork, to ensure the class itself as a whole was successful.

When I was asked how I would write a narrative or outline, my life after much thought, I would offer the following: I was born and raised in Sayreville, New Jersey. I graduated from Sayreville High School in 1958. I continued my education by attending Pennsylvania Military College 1958 through 1962. I worked two summers in various positions for DuPont in Parlin, New Jersey. After graduation in June 1962, and until March of 1963, I was employed by the United States Army Corps of Engineers, Philadelphia Engineer District, as a civil engineer. I resided in an apartment on the University of Pennsylvania campus with three former Pennsylvania Military College classmates. During that period, I was fortunate to meet my future wife at the Army Corps office. We started dating in November 1962 and after receiving my orders for active duty with an assignment to Germany, we were engaged on February 14, 1963.

I reported for active duty in March of 1963 at Fort Belvoir, Virginia, to attend Engineering Basic Officer School. I decided to get married following basic school, before departing for Nelligen, Germany, with an assignment to the Ninety-Fourth Engineer Construction Battalion. We were married on June 8, 1963.

My wife joined me in Germany for our tour of duty. We lived in an apartment off base, owned by a local German landlord. We traveled throughout Europe and, most importantly, our oldest daughter was born in Stuttgart Army Hospital in May of 1964. My wife and my daughter returned to the United States in January 1965 and I completed my tour and returned home by US troop ship in March 1965. I was discharged at Fort Hamilton, New York. The remainder of my military obligation was fulfilled by assignment to a reserve unit in Philadelphia, Pennsylvania, until my discharge in June of 1968.

We purchased a home in Drexel Hill, Pennsylvania, and I returned to work for the Philadelphia Engineer District. Our other two children, a daughter and a son, born in 1965 and 1967, arrived while I worked in various assignments until a promotion opportunity was offered in the Office of the Chief of Engineers in Washington. DC. In October 1970, I accepted the challenge and moved my family to Crofton, Maryland. My position in the corps headquarters was to manage and administer the corps programs and policies for disaster preparedness, disaster assistance, and relief and recovery following natural disasters. This position was quite rewarding and certainly very demanding of my time, in both the office and in the field locations. In June 1980, the responsibility for corps planning and preparedness activities for military contingencies was assigned to me. My background and training was a great asset to fulfill my responsibilities and obligations while I held this position.

A significant event in my life occurred in December of 1982 when I completed a senior executive education program at the Federal Executive Institute in Charlottesville, Virginia. This process was an intensive reflection on my past values and accomplishments with a view towards developing future goals and objectives in both my personal and professional life. This experience resulted in refocusing my priorities to family first, work second. Although change is never easy, these priorities have been in place since then.

In June 1985, I was promoted to Deputy Chief, Operations and Readiness Division of Civil Works. This position expanded my responsibilities to many other functional areas, i.e., navigation, regulatory permits, and natural resource management at corps facilities. In June 1989, I decided that after twenty-seven years, I would accept the early retirement package that was being offered.

After a summer of job hunting, I accepted a position as Project Manager for the State of Maryland Department of Natural Resources in October 1989.

During my ten-year career with the Department of Natural Resources, I worked on two major projects: the Ocean City, Maryland, Hurricane and Shore Protection Project and the Rocky Gap Lodge and Golf Resort in western Maryland. Both projects were a challenge to my project-management skills. The Rocky Gap Project was most diversified, since the initial planning and development required obtaining a private source for financial investment, then coordination and financial contributions from local and county government and design coordination with consultants and architect and engineering firms as well as state agencies. Finally, the construction phase was impacted by price increases, and the golf course took an additional year to complete due to weather. Again, my previous experience was an essential asset to ensure the completion of these projects. In January 2000, I resigned from the Department of Natural Resources to work with a Maryland-based construction company that specialized in golf-course construction and renovation work. I was assigned as a project engineer and administrator for a nine-hole golf course under contract to General Motors in Clark, New Jersey. In August 2001, I decided to retire, without any aspirations to return to full-time work.

My wife and I continue to reside in Crofton, Maryland, with our three children and eight grandchildren who live nearby. We enjoy traveling to the Caribbean regularly and play golf often with the seniors at Crofton Country Club. Overall, I have been blessed with a wonderful wife of forty-one years, good health, successful careers, and a beautiful family. The real tragedies that I have experienced were the passings of my father in 1972, my sister in 1985, my wife's father in 2003, and my mother in 2003.

Cadet #245
William Arthur Izzard

William Arthur Izzard

Wow, when I think about why I enrolled Pennsylvania Military College, it certainly wasn't the low cost. It certainly wasn't the freedom and fun. And, in 1962, it wasn't because Pennsylvania Military College was nationally ranked as an academic powerhouse. When I applied, I thought the idea of a uniform was neat. The college brochure hooked me. Pennsylvania Military College was far enough away to be out from under my father and my mother, but close enough to go home when I could. When my acceptance letter arrived, I actually became the first of the family to attend college, both in my family homeland of Ireland and here in America. How could I not be anxious to succeed? Little did I know what lay ahead or how I would react to the certain pressures to follow. I regretted enrolling only once, in September 1958, when the push-ups following "Second Corridor Step Out" uttered by a cadet senior officer competed with studying for a test the next day. This was my first lesson in multitasking.

When I think about significant events, the Boardwalk Bowl in Atlantic City, New Jersey, comes to mind. Then there was the fact that my first squad leader could find an error in the formula for water and blame the error on a rook. Perhaps not significant as events go, but to me, getting past my squad leader's inspections in ranks was significant. Returning to PMC as a third classman was key. I saw what I had been through from a different perspective. I felt proud that I had accomplished things which I did not believe myself capable of completing. It taught me a lot about leadership, motivation, guts, drive, and humility. Summer camp, complete with poison ivy, makes the list of significant events between my junior and senior years. I also remember the chemistry professors who wondered why I chose chemistry as a major. Also making the memories list are the mom-and-pop hoagie shops, the graduation commissioning ceremony, the leadership style of one of the captains in ROTC. I will always recall the differing leadership styles of the commandant of the cadets, the first officer, and the executive officer. Saturday home football games were a big deal. We put Pennsylvania Military College on the map, and our star fullback was the map maker. Pledging and being accepted into Theta Chi allowed me to feel a sense of belonging and got me thinking about what brotherhood really meant. I feel that same camaraderie with the Class of 1962. We have all gone different directions but have never lost touch with our nucleus of success and the values Pennsylvania Military College taught us.

I entered Pennsylvania Military College, as most eighteen- or nineteen-year-olds going to college, unsure of what lay ahead but knowing it would be difficult. My confidence in my own abilities was either unknown or lacking. I had never before assessed my own strengths and weaknesses. Well, that had to change rapidly. At Pennsylvania Military College, I soon discovered that each of us needed a set of core values to not only survive but move ahead. The cadets in your squad, platoon, and company were your classmates, but some were your sponsors and some were your mentors. I don't believe this feeling of teamwork would have existed in a civilian institution. So many of the things we were compelled to do as cadets required a focus, a discipline, and a strong feeling of not wanting to look weak in the eyes of our classmates; that is why I tried harder than I have ever tried in my life. Selfishly, I also believed that the uniform gave me a sense of identity I had previously lacked. So how did I change? Bottom line, confidence; I did something many could not do. I could lead, follow, and contribute. Pennsylvania Military College taught unity of effort and in doing so caused all of us as individuals to grow mentally and emotionally.

My four years at Pennsylvania Military College influenced my military outlook by giving me a career of which I could be proud. In twenty-six years, I achieved the rank of colonel and commanded company, battalion, and brigade levels. In fact, I loved command and being held accountable, which were factors I would have shunned in high school. I believe the discipline and the focus at Pennsylvania Military College gave me the confidence to handle combat in my two Vietnam tours. I had not planned on an Army career, but my first tour of duty in Germany following airborne school at Fort Benning, Georgia, convinced me that the Army was a great career. I am confident that I would not have felt this way had Pennsylvania Military College not structured my thinking and given me the confidence to lead soldiers. I saw good examples of leadership and staff coordination, and I saw a lot of horrible ones. Pennsylvania Military College required all of us to look beyond ourselves and in so doing to lay the groundwork for each of my future successes.

In my recent professional life as a financial planner and in other executive capacities, I have held positions in professional organizations. Pennsylvania Military College leadership and planning requirements made the task of handling the professional organizations easier. Manage things, lead people. Don't quit. I learned that early. In the business world, it paid off. The only hard transition was going from leading three thousand people in a brigade to leading one (me). But I had the confidence to look forward and the sense not to longingly look back.

With regards to my personal life, I don't know if Pennsylvania Military College caused me to turn out differently than I would have otherwise. But it did teach me to do the honorable thing and serve as a role model to those around me. It taught me personal pride and never to act in a way to bring discredit on my family.

There are many pleasant moments at Pennsylvania Military College, although none of them were life altering or provided a big aha. But to list them: end of rook period; winning the Francis M. Tate Award; good news on the make list; seeing old friends return the following year; the Boardwalk Bowl; town line formations; end of finals—eight times; the Junior Ring Dance; home football games; the final beer call at summer camp and Indian Town Gap; acing a Saturday-morning inspection; being accepted into Theta Chi; returning as cadre just before the senior year began; graduation and commissioning; actually seeing my name on a Bachelor of Science degree and the pride showing on my parents' faces; late-evening canteen runs for steak-and-cheese hoagies; receiving the monthly ROTC check; and finally completing the removal of all of the lacquer from all of my brass. They seem rather insignificant now, but at the time, they were my world.

In retrospect, I learned that something doesn't need to be monumental or momentous to make one feel good. It merely needs to please oneself. Look at the small things in life and welcome them. Some never see them and go through life feeling unlucky or thinking, *Why me*. When I add up all the little stuff delivered in nibbles, the end result is clearly a big bite out of life. Finally, I learned not to sit back after a pleasant event and think I had arrived. Surely a downer is lurking not far away. Be ready to deal with it.

I cannot honestly say that I had a worst memory other than the agony of waiting for grades and discovering that my fears were either not as grim as I thought or were dead wrong given the actual result. In a more important sense, it was always sad to see a fellow cadet not return the next semester. Humorously, my one and only tour was a blow to my ego. I felt like marching it incognito with a paper bag over my head. While this was an unpleasant experience, it was also a "suck it up and move on" moment. One other point, losing on the senior porch mess inspection, either because I was caught unprepared or was not diligent because I expected to win, was a decidedly unpleasant moment. Come to think of it, this loss was followed by counseling and supplemental leadership guidance administered by my chain of command. It didn't fade from memory quickly or easily.

Very simply, I learned three things from my unpleasant memories: First, admit your error and try not to repeat it. Second, don't let it get you down; control your attitude. Third, put it into perspective; don't get treed by a Chihuahua.

Oddly, the people who made the greatest impact on my life were not necessarily the closest friends. They were the people I looked up to, tried to copy, and tried to be like. Conversely, the clowns I have met along the way, the lazy, the dishonest, the unprincipled have taught me just as much about what not to be. Pennsylvania Military College had some of both. And because we were so structured, the good and the bad ones stood out more clearly than they would have in a civilian institution. I never developed a particularly strong bond with any one cadet but looked upon several as people I could rely on or who would give me straight, unvarnished advice when I needed it whether I asked for it or not. I guess those several cadets, as a group, became my first board of directors and mentors.

I did not know what a mentor was then, but in looking back, one of my chemistry professors, two of my classmates, and one upperclassman from the Class of 1961 were real mentors. I think that the recognition of what they did for me has caused me to mentor others, especially in my military career and to an even greater extent in my post-retirement career as a financial representative in a sales environment. Rejection comes hard to all of us, but especially hard to the novice trying to establish a successful sales career. They need mentors, and Pennsylvania Military College started me on the road to becoming one.

I erred in not attending past reunions. Part of the problem was telling someone where I was. Nineteen moves in twenty-six years tend to make one wonder who to report to. The forty-second class reunion was the first of many future reunions for me. Maybe I will "water the flowers." I attended the forty-second reunion as my first reunion initially because I was curious about how we all fared to date. But as the reunion continued, curiosity gave way to renewing fond, sometimes emotional, memories (the dance decorating committees, the home games, company competition day, rook tag removal, my first tour, one on one on Second Corridor, Howell Hall 1958, the railroad tie engineering project, the hunger strike, and Captain D as the Saturday-morning inspection officer). We went through more trials than an average college student, and my fond recollection of people long past makes me understand better who I am today. The Class of 1962 to a large extent shaped my thoughts and my success. It took me this first reunion to fully realize it. Thank you all.

I did not intend to make a career of the Army, but it worked out that way following my initial tour of duty in Germany, 1963–1966. As a tank platoon leader, company executive officer, and company commander, I enjoyed the responsibility. I studied German in high school and college and utilized it in Germany. In fact, it was largely responsible for my meeting my wife of almost forty years. Best thing that ever happened to me. Things then came into focus. My future seemed a bit more directed. Fort Polk, Louisiana, followed Germany. The swamps almost drove my wife back to Germany, and unbelievably, an inept lieutenant colonel almost drove me to become a civilian.

Life is like a sine curve. Ups will surely follow downs. The advanced course and my first tour in Vietnam followed. It was in the Republic of Vietnam that I developed a real appreciation for life as an American and for the solid support of my loving wife. A tour as a test project officer at the Armor and Engineer Board at Fort Knox, Kentucky, followed. It was here that I selected my secondary specialty of research and development. I enjoyed working with experimental equipment, some of which, thank God, never made it into the inventory. I returned to the Republic of Vietnam in the Central Highlands, but this time as a major.

As the war ended in 1973, myself and about two hundred other field grades were chosen to remain and become part of the Four Party Joint Commission on POW exchanges and ceasefire violation investigations. All others went home. We stayed. I was on the second-to-last plane out in 1973. Onward I went to recruiting duty in Baltimore, Maryland. Not a happy time. While I was proud of the uniform, few others were. A confrontation with Father Berrigan and Sister McAllister (two staunch anti-war activists) was memorable. Command and Staff College at the Naval War College in Newport, Rhode Island, followed. It was the most fun I had on any tour, apart from my command. I returned again to Germany as a tank battalion executive with a promotion to lieutenant colonel and command of a battalion. I returned back to Carlisle Barracks in Pennsylvania in 1981 as a student at the United States Army War College and was awarded my graduate degree. I then went on to the Pentagon as chief of the Foreign Science and Technology Division in OACSI. Liver patch, foreign travel often with my wife, interface with members of Congress and industry, and long days made a three-year tour memorable. Selection for colonel and brigade command at Fort Stewart, Georgia, with the Twenty-Fourth Infantry Division followed a short tour back at Fort Knox. I retired in 1989 and went to work immediately for Northwestern Mutual Life in Savannah, Georgia, as a special agent.

We built our first home and rapidly adapted to civilian life. In looking back over my twenty-six years in the United States Army and almost fifteen years with Northwestern Mutual, I have no regrets. Stay busy. Stay fit. Serve your community. Look back only to draw on lessons learned, not to long for the good old days. Yesterday is history. Tomorrow is uncertain. Today is a gift. That's why I call it the present. Pennsylvania Military College nudged me down my chosen path and gave me the tools to make the best of the cards I was dealt. I am in its debt.

The sixties was an unsettling era in our history, marked by a lack of patriotism, a self-centered desire to "do our own thing," and a hatred or distrust of all people not like us—prejudice and racism. Our class came from all backgrounds and nationalities. Our single most important tie then and now is unity: first to get through rook, next to develop a class character, and finally to leave our mark on the college history—academically, humorously, athletically, patriotically, mischievously, but above all, together as "Band of Brothers." It is evident today in the reunion camaraderie that bridged the resident, "day hop," and civilian pillars of our class.

Finally, to the author who is writing this book, all of the above was thought-provoking. I am younger than when I began. Thank you for helping me to reflect on my many blessings. And I look forward to reading the final product, *Who Will Water the Flowers?*

Cadet #339
John Nothwang

John William Nothwang Jr.

The primary factor leading to my enrolling at Pennsylvania Military College, simply stated, was a desire to prepare for a military career. There is more to this story, given the unique aspects of the Class of 1962; there is a serendipitous aspect to my ending up there. Some might call it fate, others as God's leading. While my primary concern was to prepare for a military career, Pennsylvania Military College was not on my immediate radar screen. I knew I would not be able to obtain an appointment to a service academy and became enamored with the prospect of attending Virginia Military Institute. That proved not to be an option, as my dad was very opposed to a Yankee heading into a southern educational military environment, and he thought Lexington, Virginia, was too far from our home in Pittsburgh, Pennsylvania. Ironically, Chester, Pennsylvania, is in fact farther from Pittsburgh, but that didn't matter. The fiancé of my girlfriend's sister was attending Pennsylvania Military College, and that connection led to our visiting and my decision to attend.

I remember my initial meeting with Mr. Huntsinger in a Pittsburgh hotel to discuss the school, and then traveling by train with my dad to visit and take an entrance examination. This was followed by the measuring of uniforms at Bells, the orientation process, my pride in being a cadet, my disappointment when General Mac Moreland retired and was replaced by a nonmilitary president. I became aware that as much as I liked Pennsylvania Military College, it was not regarded with the same respect as places like Virginia Military Institute and the Citadel. Still, being with great guys to share life impacting experiences helped me to realize I could do more and tolerate more than I ever imagined.

I had a unique and troubling experience that defines, in some way, the dichotomy that existed. I attended a college that would punish prevarication but tolerated at least one faculty member who violated principles of good conduct. Our faculty advisor for Theta Chi overrode my decision as president. I ruled not to allow the showing of pornographic movies in our fraternity house. I remember feeling the fraternity would be in trouble if we were caught engaging in this unbecoming conduct. Yet he imposed his values on what I felt was my responsibility. He pulled rank on me.

I think there are many changes as an individual that took place in my attendance over four years at Pennsylvania Military College. I think these changes would not have occurred had I not enrolled in a college with a military environment. I attained a level of self-confidence that I see as different from that which would have evolved as a natural part of the maturing process in a nonmilitary environment.

I gained the capacity to cope with stress, particularly that stemming from what was on the surface was pure nonsense. I learned to see beyond the apparent and seek the practical in the seemingly absurd. I further developed a keen sense of owning principles and to loyalty to principles, comrades in arms, and colleagues. There is no doubting that I was sharpened in many ways. Pennsylvania Military College offered its joys and sorrows, and I learned to accept both and keep on going. The quote "When the going gets tough, the tough get going" is applicable as part of this change. The concept of the Corps of Cadets is a factor in all I learned and in all I tried.

There is a sense of accomplishment in having journeyed through a relatively unique experience. Ultimately, I achieved my goal of graduating and being commissioned, because I wanted it and the system required that I do it on its terms.

A contrast comes to mind in a then-versus-now culture; in today's environment, something is always someone else's fault. We learned to accept the consequences of our actions and never quit.

As I look back over my four years at Pennsylvania Military College, I had the following specific influences in my life in the following areas: In my military career I found it easy to perform at a high level compared to those from nonmilitary environments, and I found it very difficult to tolerate standards differing from that which I felt were appropriate. My professional life outside of the military required far more discipline, tenacity, conscientiousness, and loyalty to and respect for authority, particularly when I disagreed with it. And finally, in my personal life and in interpersonal relationships with family and friends, I am known as dedicated, disciplined, particular about personal appearance, fiercely loyal, and a leader.

My most pleasant memories and experiences at Pennsylvania Military College consisted of my friends, surviving the system, rising above the circumstances, Theta Chi, the joy of the beginning there, and the joy of leaving there. I won't ever forget earning a varsity swimming letter, weekends with cadet buddies, and hop weekends. What I learned from all of this is that relationships are important and loyalty and discipline are foundational values that pay great dividends in all aspects of my life.

I recall some of my worst memories and experiences at Pennsylvania Military College. I was demoted because of academic probation, and it seemed to follow me even after the situation was corrected. I had some health issues in my sophomore year. So what did I learn from these memories and experiences? Suck it up and get over it.

There are many of my classmates during their early years who contemplated transferring from Pennsylvania Military College to another school. There were events that led me to some thoughts of considering leaving Pennsylvania Military College to join the Marines rather than attend another school. I liked the military routine far better than the academic classes, and I felt the Marines would provide the military career I aspired to. I did not pursue joining the Marines because of the high value my dad placed on a college education. His opposition was particularly fueled by the fact that he lacked a college education. My fiancé was opposed also, so it boiled down to a choice of the Marines or her. Since that marriage ended in divorce, perhaps I should have picked the Marines.

I must say, I particularly admire the cadet brother who did join the Marines. In addition, my friendship with Cadet #224 had the greatest impact on me. He ended up being my next-door neighbor in California and was instrumental in my attaining a position with Ford Motor Company. This proved to be a very successful career move.

The reason reunions are important to me and why I attend is that they are great for remembering the good and for laughing at the less-positive times. I truly enjoy reliving times and connecting with those with whom I was close and with those who were not my buddies at that time. I value greatly my Pennsylvania Military College experience and enjoy my connections to it.

When I look back and think of a narrative as to how I would outline my life, I think I would have to start with my greatest strength is my trust in others, and my greatest weakness is my trust in others. If I were to define three relationships that have significantly impacted my life, they are my first wife, my present wife of twenty-four years, and my personal relationship with Jesus Christ. Each of these relationships has made, broken, or shaped me in no small measure. While time is long past for fixing blame, my first marriage was the prime reason (although there were many other factors) for my leaving the military.

This was a marriage to a high school sweetheart that lasted thirteen years, produced two daughters, and fell apart. This must number as a major failure in my life. Where and when failure developed is difficult to judge, but I do mark it as failure. Through the divorce I became far more independent and self-sufficient. The context for this is I had never lived alone, home to Pennsylvania Military College to marriage, so I found it exhilarating to discover I was very effective and comfortable on my own.

After five years of being single, I accepted a blind date and was married eleven months later. What a delightful discovery a good marriage has proven to be. My standard comment is that "I am blessed because of my wife and in spite of me." This relationship is the most significant in my life from an earthly standpoint: a wonderful mother to my children from the previous marriage, and in every respect a valued life partner and my best friend. She is also a major factor in the process of developing the singularly most significant relationship in my life, that with Jesus Christ. This relationship has replaced all concepts of values and ethics with his absolute truth for living life to the fullest. From a career standpoint, I have had three distinct endeavors: the automotive industry, banking, and the ministry. Each has been successful in its own right, and all predicated on characteristics that in some measure were honed at Pennsylvania Military College. These characteristics are honesty, drive, integrity, loyalty, and relationships.

I hold strongly to the loyalty in every form of relationship; integrity at its core is who you are when no one is looking, and it is not a characteristic that is occasional.

I think that, like myself, many of us journeyed to Pennsylvania Military College somewhat circuitously. Should this prove to be true, then there was a crossing of life's paths of like-minded young men who arrived in the fall of 1958 unarmed and left four years later with a quiver of unique experiences to carry them through life. I believe we share pride in the journey and, a penchant for honesty, integrity, grit, and looking back. We realized who we were [and] who led us there, and in the foundry of cadet life, we were shaped to live lives of purpose.

Cadet #363
George Shaffer

George Courtney Shaffer

During my senior year in high school, many thoughts were racing through my mind about college. I was familiar with the Army because my father served at the end of the Second World War and during the Korean conflict. My aim was to attend military college and make the Army a career. Fortunately, I enjoyed football and achieved some success in high school as a fullback. Because I made two touchdowns during a game, I received a TV sports award as outstanding football player of the week and appeared on a local sports show. By happenstance, George Hansell, head football coach and athletic director at Pennsylvania Military College, was also on the show and he invited me to the campus. A cadet major showed me around, and I was very impressed. Weeks later, the football coach from the Citadel came to my home and offered me a scholarship, but I would have to attend prep school first.

My academic abilities did not match my ability to get my head bashed in on the football field. Money for college was a significant issue; however, my father was a physician and he made the choice for me to attend Pennsylvania Military College. Penn State was also an option, but I would have to have been required to be a physical education major, much to the chagrin of my father. So on a hot August day, I climbed the steps of Old Main to report for football camp with these words from my father: "These will be the greatest days of your life." How insightful and correct he was.

All my experiences at Pennsylvania Military College remain vivid in my memory as compared to other periods of my life, perhaps because of the chemistry I shared with my fellow cadets. Freshman year was the most challenging experience because of the "rook" year, as it was called. It was also a blast.

Sophomore year was difficult. My grades were not great, and the draft board was breathing down my neck. I was interviewed by Mr. Taylor and Clarence R. Moll. They said they would bear with me and were supportive. During that year, I considered transferring to a number of different schools, but the civilian interest, concern, and support I received at Pennsylvania Military College was wonderful. Football was OK, but George Hansell, football coach and athletic director, was not as supportive as others. I played and received a varsity letter but felt lost.

Some of the guys on the football team were Korean vets, older than the rest of us. I talked to them, and they said, "Hang in there," as did many other of my classmates.

During the year, the entire class was required to take the RQ Five exam in order to be accepted into ROTC. It was a big event. I gave it my best effort but did not pass. The required score was 112, I received 111. Colonel Bennett, Commandant of Cadets, had the ability to grant a waiver. He didn't like my attitude or something, because he denied my request as well as the request of my father. Well, my dream of a military career went down the old rathole. By this time, I had seen many of my classmates receive special orders and take the punishment, restrictions, march tours and not falter. The end of my sophomore year showed some hope academically, but it was back to summer school with the hope of getting a 2.0 GPA so that I could get off campus in my junior year and be able to graduate at the end of my senior year. I took a Study and Reading course with Eleanor Logan at the library, and surprise, surprise, she determined I had a real reading and comprehension problem and poor study skills. Her insight helped me immensely, and my grades improved. I made a 2.0 GPA in my junior year.

Sophomore and junior years were filled with fraternity activities and football, which was going well. I received a lot of support from my classmates during football season.

I pledged Delta Delta Rho, which later became TKE. I was the historian in my junior year. Since I was not in ROTC, I became a "Slater waiter" and loved every minute of it. It allowed me to miss formations and wear gray khakis and a jacket. I became very friendly with the kitchen staff. The head chef, John, and I would joke every day about football and other things. After my parents attended the little Army–Navy game where we played against Kings Point Academy in Atlantic City, New Jersey, they would frequently remark about the kitchen staff telling them "He's our boy." I loved it.

My junior year was great: 2.0 grade point average, weekends, ring dance, and airport motel. It could not get any better. I was encouraged by my classmates to run for class president for my senior year. I was humbled by winning the election. To this day, I consider this one of the most significant events at Pennsylvania Military College. I realized during the election the secret of the Class of 1962 was its brotherhood. Football was always big in my youth. In my junior year, our line coach, Rock Royer, asked me to switch to the guard position because the offense needed a pulling guard with speed and he thought I filled the bill. It was a great move. Everything was going well in my senior year. I made A&R sergeant for Company Echo and was class president. Law school was in my plans, and I needed very good grades. One of my classmates offered to help me. He had a consistent 3.0 GPA throughout college. I visited his room often to have him underline the important passages in the textbook and tell me what the professor would possibly think was important. The help was terrific.

I told the author of this book that I remembered listening to "Please Mr. Postman" until the needle wore out. The Chevrons had retired by that time.

The ring dance was very significant. The choice and type of ring was very important at the beginning of the year, and then the culmination at the dance. The choice of an orchestra was most interesting. Two of my fellow senior classmates campaigned for Maynard Ferguson of Canada. At the end of the dance, Colonel Bennett, the commandant of cadets, approached the bandstand and asked Maynard Ferguson to play the Star-Spangled Banner. Maynard Ferguson asked Colonel Bennett to hum a few bars of it. Then he played it beautifully.

Senior year was a culmination of a building process. The anticipated plan was proceeding well. The traditional one hundred days banquet was a real success. I had the required credits to graduate and had been accepted at the University of West Virginia Law School. Another one of my senior classmates and I were going there together. So what could go wrong?

I was living on the third floor of Turrell Hall when an underclassman came into my room and asked what the seniors were building on the street in front of Old Main. I hurried over to the room of two of my other senior classmates and saw some of my classmates (never to be named) taking railroad ties off the campus truck and methodically building twin towers on either side of the street with a banner saying, "Welcome PTA." The next day was the annual traditional Parents' Day, with many events planned throughout the day for visiting parents. At the end of the day, we would usually go off campus for dinner with our parents or for the rest of the weekend if your grade point average permitted. About twelve to twenty cadet seniors participated in the twin tower project. No underclassmen were permitted to take part. It was a substantial edifice. The railroad ties had been taken from a site at the lower end of the athletic field. They had been there for about a week prior to the twin tower construction project. They were irresistible temptations to some of my classmates. It was a spring evening, just before graduation. I must share with you now so you understand that after six p.m., the campus was run by the seniors with officer of the day and guard duty. As could be anticipated, Saturday morning came bright and early, and all hell broke loose. Colonel Bennett, Commandant of Cadets, and President Clarence R. Moll wanted the towers disassembled. They summoned the senior officers, who refused to remove the twin towers. The college maintenance staff was assigned to remove the towers so embarrassment for the administration was avoided. As class president and the vice president of the senior class were summoned to President Clarence R. Moll's office, I was asked to give him the names of the seniors involved in the misdeed and responded by telling him the whole class was responsible. I knew that President Clarence R. Moll understood, but Colonel Bennett, Commandant of Cadets, thought it was a breach of military discipline. The order came down that all seniors were restricted until further notice. Many parents were disappointed and many plans were abandoned.

Sunday evening, we had many small meetings in Howell Hall regarding what our next move would be. It was decided that no names would be given. We decided to begin a hunger strike at mess. Bill's Hoagie Shop, pizza shops, and others began record sales that night. On Monday after first mess, when much food had been wasted, things really began to escalate. The *Philadelphia Enquirer* and TV outlets as well as the New York papers were beginning to call the school regarding the issue. I was called again to President Clarence R. Moll's office to give the names of the involved seniors, at which time I declined to do. It was at this point that we were told there would be no graduation, no commission, and no Class of 1962. No food was consumed at second mess by any seniors or juniors, who were supporting us. The senior class was called to the auditorium and addressed by President Clarence R. Moll and Colonel Bennett, Commandant of Cadets. They wanted the names. They left us so we could discuss the situation. The meeting began with much discussion, but the decision that the entire Class of 1962 responsible and the giving of no names would prevail. President Clarence R. Moll and Colonel Bennett, Commandant of Cadets, returned. Colonel Bennett asked those responsible to stand up and confess their misdeed. It took more than an hour with several intervals for the entire class to stand up and declare, "We, the Class of 1962, are responsible." Colonel Bennett's face went white. We continued to be confined to campus but ceased the hunger strike. The kitchen staff was obligated to prepare and provide food for the cadets, and that the fact that it was being wasted heavily weighed on us. Also, we were getting really tired of hoagies and pizzas. During the next couple of days, I was summoned to President Clarence R. Moll's office. Eventually, he suggested that if the Class of 1962 wrote a letter of apology, it would likely be accepted with comment and the incident would be resolved. President Clarence R. Moll in turn wrote a letter to our parents indicating that the Class of 1962 accepted responsibility for the incident, and apologized for its consequences, and gave assurance that their future action would be in accordance with acceptable standards for first classmen. He finally ended the letter by announcing that the restrictions had been removed and the senior cadets had returned to good standing. Graduation was back on.

At some time—I can't recall if it was while we were still in school or later as I continued to see President Clarence R. Moll at college events—I learned that he really wanted to resolve the situation very early on and had admiration for the Class of 1962's unity but Colonel Bennett, Commandant of Cadets, would not budge.

I see this is a perfect example of the bond that had been formed over four years. My thought was that it was purely a college prank. No lies were told, and for all those responsible, the whole Class of 1962 accepted responsibility.

As an individual, I became very resourceful. I learned how to accomplish tasks under high pressure. I learned how a small unit of roommates can accomplish a great deal. I saw how you must rely on others to help push the ball ahead. To act alone is the most difficult way to achieve goals. I really grew to know the need for team play outside of athletic endeavors. If I had attended a civilian college, it would have been more "me" centered.

I was so unhappy at graduation because I would no longer be living with my classmates.

My professional life reflected lessons learned at Pennsylvania Military College: ability to work with other people and exchange ideas and debate resolutions, meticulous personal appearance and diligence, which is almost compulsion. I learned that being part of a unit that worked like a well-oiled machine was terrific.

The one major downside of my pleasant memories and experiences was my worst memory of not being granted a waiver by Colonel Bennett, Commandant of Cadets, for one point on the RQ5 exam, which kept me from participating in ROTC, which was the primary reason I attended Pennsylvania Military College.

Reunions are great. As president of the Alumni Association, I had responsibilities during reunion weekends. The Class of 1962 always had a great reputation as being a really tight group of men. We were one of the top classes in participation and giving to the annual alumni fundraising. The administration never knew what to expect from us. At one reunion, we were going to Jack's Tavern from the hotel on a school bus and decided to stop at President Bob Bruce's house. We piled off the bus and approached President Bruce at his door, telling him how great it was to be invited, and then said we were just joking, much to his relief. At another reunion, we invited President Clarence R. Moll and his wife Ruth to sit with our class and be in our class picture. At one of the broom drills at the new stadium, when I was carrying the guidon, we formed our own company and someone gave the order "To the rear march." Our company turned and left the other classes in the broom drill. This is part of the essence of the class and, combined with the ability to pick up with each other where we left off either from 1962 or the reunion, demonstrates the bond we established so long ago. Status and wealth never seem to have an effect on our relationships. I have been to many reunions, and few classes can match our unity.

I remember meeting one of my fellow senior classmates in Old Main in our freshman year. He was very military in his bearing. He had, and still to this day has, the ability to tell a good story. He has had many life experiences and has an excellent perspective. We became great friends at Pennsylvania Military College, enjoyed summer school together, and trips to another one of our fellow classmates' home in New York. He and his wife had retired to Maryville, Tennessee, and developed a great friendship. He has since been called home by God.

As I indicated earlier, in my senior year, I, along with one of my senior fellow classmates, was accepted at the University of West Virginia Law School and decided to share an apartment. Although I didn't stay in West Virginia, we remain close friends. We later formed a corporation to buy some land together for commercial development. I was in his wedding and watched his family grow and grow up while we visited over the years. We would all go out on my boat when they visited us in Fort Meyers, Florida. He and I also played our own Wimbledon tennis tournament for a few years. At the time of this writing, we had just attended one of their daughters' engagement parties and saw them at Christmastime. His lovely wife and my lovely wife have become friends as well.

If any of you who are taking this journey would ask me the question how would I outline my life thus far, I would share with you the following. I initially attended the University of West Virginia Law School for one semester. I transferred to the University of Baltimore Law School and graduated in 1965. Throughout law school, I had a part-time job as a "house parent" at Boy's Home Society, a residential facility for teenagers court-ordered to live there. I shared an apartment with another law school student and lived next door, to my surprise, to my future bride. I mistakenly parked my car in her paid-for parking space, which caused her to contact me to resolve the situation. To this day, she is still trying to resolve the situation.

I worked for the law school following graduation, took the Maryland Bar Exam unsuccessfully, married in January 1967, and reported for an Army physical in March 1967. Fortunately, I was too old for them by then. I went to work in the real estate department for Cities Service Oil Company, securing and disposing of service-station sites from Maryland to New Jersey. My wife and I then moved from Baltimore, Maryland, to Bensalem, Pennsylvania, to work for a private real estate broker that I had met through my work for Cities Service. I started my own real estate company in 1973, and we had previously bought our first house in 1971. There were two to five employees in my company during these years. It was primarily a residential practice with some land and commercial sales. I became active in the Pennsylvania Military College Alumni Association, becoming president of the Board of Managers at one point. I attended many football games and college activities. I attended the retirement of the colors ceremony and watched the college and campus take on a dramatic change under the leadership of President Clarence R. Moll. The college became a university, and a law school was established in Delaware. I finally closed the real estate business, and we decided to head to the Sunshine State. Two reasons for the move were the miserable northeast weather and the real estate opportunities in southwest Florida. While establishing myself as a real estate broker, I worked for a local broker, then for a Canadian development company before again opening my own business in 1983. The business was primarily commercial, office, and industrial leasing and sales and commercial and office building management. I had identified a need in the local counties for this service, and I am glad to say I met those needs and proved very successful. I maintained contact with some of my former classmates and would enjoy visits from some of them during those years.

Following serious illnesses for my wife (breast cancer) and myself (heart attack) between November 1996 and March 1997, we evaluated our lives and decided we would like to leave hot, humid weather and ever-more crowded Lee County, Florida, for a less hectic lifestyle and started looking and learning about a variety of places. Fortunately, we had the ability to retire early and only have to concern ourselves with where to live and not about where to work. We visited east Tennessee on several occasions and after considerable research decided to reside in Maryville, Tennessee, where we currently enjoy our lives.

Cadet #383
John Tysall

John Michael Tysall

My enrollment in Pennsylvania Military College was predicated by time and place. I was three years out of high school and I knew I needed a structured environment to achieve academic growth. My initial recollection of the significant events at Pennsylvania Military College take me back to my interface with college students, coaches, and teachers, and participation in intercollegiate athletics.

I think I changed as an individual during my four years of attendance at Pennsylvania Military College. I grew mentally and sought information in subject areas that were previously unexplored. These changes were different from those that would have occurred had I attended a nonmilitary college. I believe the nonmilitary environment would have offered more time to be less goal-directed.

Unique factors contributed to personal change at Pennsylvania Military College, and they had a specific influence on my life in two areas. Initially, my military training prepared me for being a commissioned officer in the United States Army and made it easy for me to take over the responsibilities of leadership both while on active duty and in the Reserves. Secondly, in my professional life outside of the military, the management techniques learned in the military are, in fact, an extension of the principles used in business. The exposure to corporate training is nothing more than a revalidation to sound military leadership techniques.

I have pleasant memories about interpersonal relationships; it was a time of bonding with my classmates. As the years have passed, we seem to have grown closer to each other as we reflect on the fact that we all experienced the same things simultaneously and a brotherhood formed despite our not realizing that it was happening.

Conversely, I can recall at least a couple of my worst memories and experiences at PMC. I realized that the administration was working against the cadets to buy time to change from a unique respected military college to a substandard, run-of-the-mill "Motel 6" training program complete with the facade of new buildings dedicated to Clarence R. Moll. The memorial was housed in the bowels of a misguided, misdirected attempt to create an engineering school. Even with this worst memory, I can honestly say I never did contemplate transferring from Pennsylvania Military College to another school.

When I first thought about what overall learnings, beliefs, and life messages I carried with me after graduation, I was not sure I took anything. But as time passed, I found myself revisiting behavior and thought processes that I learned at Pennsylvania Military College. Even to the extent of reading old textbooks, not because I had to, but because I was re-interested in the subject matter.

Friendships were formed, and I can think of several. The one that stands out is with an individual I met on the first day on campus. We both played football. He was a day cadet and I was a boarder. As the four years passed, we shared and we bonded. Upon graduation, we stayed in touch through the Alumni Association and reunions. When he got out of active-duty service, his health began to fail to the extent that he became completely dependent on his wife, caregivers. As the illness progressed, VA medical staff was necessary. In the mid- and late 1990s, every visit I could make to the east coast, I would rent a full-size car, pile him and his wheelchair in, and off to campus we would go for a half a day. I would push that chair in the rain and snow. We would visit a Middle Atlantic Championship Trophy with both of our names on it and talk about the "Gumper." He would laugh and scratch as we went to see Chris in the alumni office and try to tell her how to do her job and laugh some more. He was a positive influence on everyone who knew him—wife, children, friends, business partners—never complaining. My friend was a perfect example of that sign in the auditorium that states, "When wealth is lost, nothing is lost. When health is lost, something is lost. When character is lost, all is lost." He, his actions, and those principals of life are part of what I think about when I think about the mention of Pennsylvania Military College.

Over the span of fifty years since graduation, my working career reflected two years on active duty in the United States Army, account manager positions with Honeywell Information Systems and Management Science America, Strategic Marketing and New Business Development Manager at Motorola, Director of Worldwide Marketing at Burroughs Corporation, and several vice president positions in marketing and sales at ADP Corporation and Protech, Inc.

When I think about the past, I fully realize that what we, as cadets, went through while we were at Pennsylvania Military College was very enlightening. The late fifties and early sixties were challenging times of social change in the country. And yet, this little college in Pennsylvania laid down a foundation for us to reflect on as we went through the most trying times in the history of the country since the Revolutionary War (1960–1980).

This was a time of race-relations issues, the Russian Bear, political leaders assassinated, the 1968 conventions in Chicago, 59,000 dead in a war of no meaning, economic roller coasters, and personal struggles to raise a family, secure a career, and continue to be a good citizen. If you reflect on all of the aforementioned, our time is nearly applicable to today's headlines; just the names and places have changed. The men of the Class of 1962 were honed in the shadow of "the dome" to prepare for the stick-to, suck-it-up attitude required to constructively get through these times.

In later years, we would all speak more openly to each other about the above, yet it took time for us to express these feelings. We can see each others' reaction to the problems in our own way, and yet when they are expressed and laid end to end, the common threads are laid bare and 265 individuals collectively weave a thread and a fabric that paints a picture of what we were and what we are today.

With much sadness and a heavy heart, I share the news that Cadet #383 has crossed the bar.

Cadet #393
Glen Winn

Glen Edmund Winn

I have always had respect for the military. When I was a little boy, I lived next to Westover Air Force Base in Holyoke, Massachusetts. I went to grade school during the last two years of World War II. B-17 bombers and other military aircraft flew over my house and my school. I had second cousins that served in the Navy. I went to visit them at their various military bases. My parents taught me respect for the military. I loved parades as a child. When the war ended, I was in Milwaukee, Wisconsin, visiting with my grandparents. They took me to a huge parade on the main street of Milwaukee. I always loved war movies, John Wayne, etc.; thus began my desire to be a Marine.

I attended a Jesuit high school where one of the scholastics had been a paratrooper at Normandy. He wore a cassock but always wore his jump boots. My math teacher was in the Army and had a shaved head. I had total respect for these guys. My goal was that I gradually set my sights on attending West Point or Annapolis. I was a terrible math student and had to take special courses to pass algebra. I attended Marquette University for one year and had terrible grades. So I went to a prep school for the academy test. I was selected by my congressman to take the test for Annapolis and came in second. I was the first alternate. I then applied to Virginia Military Institute, Pennsylvania Military College, the Citadel, and Norwich University. I was accepted to all and made a decision to attend Pennsylvania Military College. Being a northern boy from Wisconsin, I was warned to not attend Virginia Military Institute or the Citadel. For obvious reasons, I had a very high level of non-prejudicial feeling towards everyone. I have tried to maintain this ethos all of my life. In Vietnam, my unit was sixty percent minorities. I brought out with me everyone that I took in.

Now back to Pennsylvania Military College. I came to PMC with some preconceived ideas that it would be as strict as West Point. So I was prepared for Rafael Nidal and Ronald Duchin. I then broke the norm and joined the Marines in January 1959. My poor mother had a stroke the night I called home and told them that I had gone to Philadelphia Navy Yard and signed up. As some remember, I was the butt of jokes of many upperclassmen. I guess this is the primary factor that made me work hard and get good grades. I was always a B or C student. Through all of this I kept my Catholic faith, which I have kept in spite of losing my first wife, to mental illness. God gave us three children, which we raised; they now have five, my grandchildren. I did marry again, and that was a disaster. Alcohol took over. That marriage ended and I stayed single until I met my present wife. I served six years in the Marines and seven years in the United States Secret Service. I went undercover for many months and was inside a Mafia organization for a while. The case was being considered and selected for a new TV show, *The Secret Service*. Then I went to work for Audrey Meadows and Bob Six at Continental Airlines. We had 121 airplanes in CAS, all in Laos and Vietnam. Then I was hired by Western Airlines for a total of four years. Then I went on to be director of Northwest Airlines and then on for seven years to United Airlines. So for fourteen years, I continued to have assignments all over the world. I was in Manila, Philippines, in 1989 when a couple of incidents and events took place. I wrote a paper for the CIA after that one. I escaped on a Philippines airliner, 747, with some of the coup leaders. I was director of security in Chicago until 1997. When I was recovering from colon cancer, I was asked to take over an office in the west and be near my family. I did move to California and have been there ever since.

The camaraderie at Pennsylvania Military College has kept me going. The phone calls from all my brothers this year have kept me going through this challenge.

One of my most memorable life events was in 1987. I was asked by the Northwest chief executive officer to take President Kim de Jung back to Korea from his self-isolation in Boston, Massachusetts. I took seven air marshals and ninety supporters, including Mary Treavors from Peter, Paul, and Mary. We flew on a Northwest Airliner, 747, from Chicago to Tokyo to Seoul. That was quite an experience. When I returned to MSP, I was debriefed.

Finally, the bottom line is that our class set precedent that is unequaled. The Marines have their corps, but we have a Band of Brothers. God bless, and take care.

With much sadness, I share the news that Cadet #383 has been called home by God.

Cadet #693
William Muehsam

William Ernest Muehsam

In 1957, my senior year in high school, I was contacted by Coach Hansell to ascertain if I would be interested in attending Pennsylvania Military College. I was a highly successful track athlete and a Pennsylvania state champion in the 100, 200, and 20 yard dashes. I thanked him for his interest but informed him that I was committed to attending the Philadelphia Museum School of Art to study advertising design. My budding artistic career was cut short because I could see that my talent level wasn't going to make me successful, so toward the end of 1957, I called Coach Hansell to see if he was still interested in me. We met and agreed that I would seek admission for fall of 1958, which I did. I was admitted and started my college career in the day cadet program in September 1958.

There is no single event that really stands out about my four years at Pennsylvania Military College. I formed many strong friendships, I immersed myself in college life, and overall it was a most congenial, uplifting experience.

One thing that I can state with certainty, I would not be the person I am today if I had not attended Pennsylvania Military College. I went from being a happy-go-lucky kid, not all that serious about my education, to a person driven and committed to succeed. Military training causes one to focus and concentrate. You lose your individualism to a great extent and gradually focus on becoming part of a greater whole. I can state, with absolute certainty, that I would not have succeeded in life to the same degree, nor acquired the same value system, had I not attended Pennsylvania Military College. Those who have never experienced a military environment cannot fully appreciate what sharing a foxhole does to you and for you. You are taught certain leadership fundamentals. You learn that you must develop vision and organizational skills. You need to have an ardent passion for any assigned task, no matter how trivial. You need to acquire the requisite technical knowledge and high energy drive. But foremost, you need to develop concern for those you expect to lead, and you need to develop and exhibit the ability to inspire competence in others. To a great degree, I first learned these skills at Pennsylvania Military College.

I cannot think of any one friendship at Pennsylvania Military College that I can say was more or less important than any other. Obviously, some impacted me positively and others impacted me in a negative manner. I had a pastor who often said we are the sum total, as a person, of all the people that have ever touched our lives, for good or for evil.

Outside of my father, the only person who impacted my life greatly was my first troop commander in the Army, Captain Don Balz. He turned me from a green second lieutenant into an effective officer in the United States Army. He is still one of my greatest heroes. I was born to a blue-collar family; my father was a welder by trade. Our family life was a happy one until I was twelve years old. My mother ran off with another man, and I was devastated. It crushed me to the point that I went from being a straight-A student in elementary school to becoming a very indifferent student in high school. When I got to college, I blossomed and became a consistent 3.0 GPA student and graduated in the upper ten percent of our class. I worked briefly after graduation but looked forward to entering the Army on active duty. After Officers Basic School at Fort Knox, Kentucky, I was posted to Schofield Barracks, Hawaii, and became a platoon leader in the Third Squadron, Fourth US Calvary. I ultimately ended up as executive officer of A Company, First Battalion, Sixty-ninth Armor. I was with that unit when the Twenty-fifth Division deployed to Vietnam. I became the company commander shortly after we arrived in country, and held that post until I was reassigned to USARV HQ as an assistant G-3.

I came home and was discharged in March 1967, when I went to work for Pennsylvania Military College in Admissions. My job was to travel the United States, visiting military prep schools and offering ROTC scholarships to seniors. There were few takers, and I believe that the death knell for the Corp of Cadets began to be sounded at that time. In the meantime, my festering hostility toward my first wife was engendered by her stubborn insistence that I resign from the Army. This finally culminated in our divorce in 1974. In 1975, I married the love of my life, Maureen. We have shared thirty-three wonderful years, and we hope for many more.

When I am asked why do I attend reunions, I say to myself and to others, Why do lemmings run to the sea every year? How do I explain this chemistry to each of you? I am not sure that I can. But I will try. I think what makes the men of the Class of 1962 unique, and special, is that we deeply care about each other. It matters little that we may not have seen you in forty-five years; if you show up, you are instantly a brother forever. To go further, I am frequently asked what makes us so special. My reply is that I am certain that we cannot define ourselves; however, the fact that other classes have acknowledged that we are exceptional is a clue. I strongly feel that the glue that binds us together is indefinable, but at the same time real. I can feel it, I can share it, but I cannot quantify it. Suffice it to say, it exists, and thank God that it does. The Class of 1962 forever.

With much sadness, I share the news that Cadet #693 has been called home by God.

Captain D
Guilio DeSerafino

GUILIO L. DiSERAFINO
Captain
Assistant Commandant

Captain D

On the day the Class of 1962 arrived at PMC, Captain D greeted us as boys. At graduation, he saluted us as men.

As rooks, we feared his authority; as we matured, we grew to love him as our leader. Each acknowledges that the personal attributes of honesty, integrity, discipline, honor, and leadership can be largely attributed to Captain D's efforts to help us mature into men and leaders. What follows are Captain D's memories.

My initial experiences at PMC were as a cadet from 1948 to 1952. From 1956 to 1962, I served as adjutant and assistant commandant of cadets.

In high school, I felt my chances of going to college were slim. I had three older brothers in college, and the financial picture for me was not good. Fortunately for me, the football coach from PMC scouted my high school. I came home after a game to find him at my house. I lived only thirty minutes from PMC, yet I had never heard of it.

Coach Woody Ludwig and I talked about football. He interviewed me with questions about family, school, sports, and social activities. Then Coach Ludwig offered me the opportunity to play football at PMC.

Following my coach's advice, I worked hard and stayed out of trouble. I lettered three years in football, baseball, and basketball. Playing sports allowed me to develop inner strength and self-discipline. I learned how to be both a team player and a leader. In my senior year, I was elected captain of the football team, appointed cadet captain of Baker Company, and served as leader of the internationally recognized drill team now known as the Pershing Rifle Drill Team.

Good friends at PMC helped me appreciate the importance of tolerance and teamwork. I was able to overcome my hotheadedness and to control my temper. I came to understand the value of true friendship. In 1952, I graduated as a distinguished military student and was commissioned a second lieutenant in the United States Army.

In 1956, I returned to PMC as a member of the commandant's staff and eventually was promoted to assistant commandant of cadets. For the next three years, I worked hard, diligently doing everything possible to maintain the integrity of the corps.

Over time, it became clear to the educational staff and I that the existence of PMC as a military institution hung in the balance. There was a shift in focus from military to civilian education in the leadership of the college. I was counseled to change careers before the change was made.

And so, I pursued a new life path.

I had attended graduate school during the 1958–1959 school year and earned a master's degree in guidance and counseling. Continuing my postgraduate education, I earned credits in school administration. When the need to change careers became apparent, I secured a position as guidance counselor at South Plainfield High School in New Jersey. Later, I accepted the same position at a high school in Pennsylvania. This led to several other positions and finally to the job of principal at Kearny High School, Kearny, New Jersey. I retired in June 1992 after serving as principal for seventeen years.

My wife, Marie, and I moved to Bonita Springs, Florida, in 1997. Sadly, after fifty-seven years of a happy marriage, Marie passed away in November 2012. I lost my partner, friend, and the mother of our two beautiful daughters. I continue to live in Bonita Springs and realize that my life has been full of wonderful times and experiences. Indeed, I have been fortunate to be part of the PMC brotherhood of cadets. I will always be grateful for the cadets who befriended my family. It has been a great privilege to know so many great men. Many continue to keep in contact with me to this day.

To the Corps of Cadets and to all my veteran friends, I offer a salute. May God's blessing be with you always.

The Class of 1962 salutes you, Captain D.

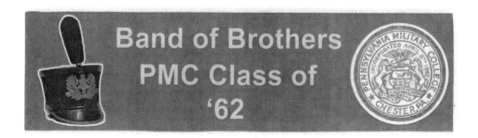

Band of Brothers
PMC Class of
'62

Cadet # 271, Louis Horner

Cadet #271, 1962, Dress Uniform

Commissioned 2nd Lieutenant

Parade Dress

President Dwight D. Eisenhower visits PMC

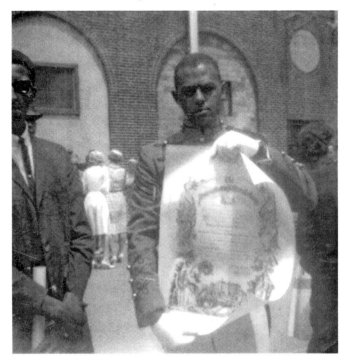

My Degree

Me and Mom, Elaine Bush

Grandpa, Pat Grant, and I

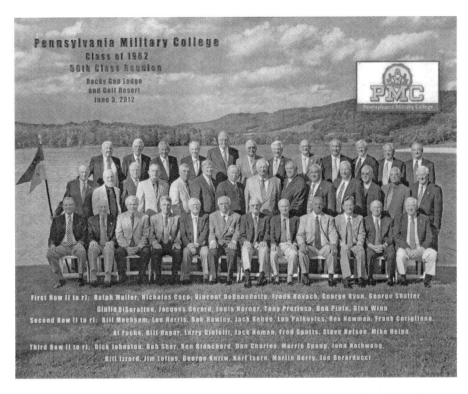

Pennsylvania Military College
Class of 1962
50th Class Reunion
Rocky Gap Lodge
and Golf Resort
June 3, 2012

First Row (l to r): Ralph Muller, Nicholas Coco, Vincent DeBenedetto, Frank Kovach, George Ryan, George Sholler
Giulio DiSerafino, Jacques Gerard, Louis Horner, Tony Prerioso, Bob Pinto, Glen Winn
Second Row (l to r): Bill Muehsam, Lou Harris, Bob Hawley, Jack Kebee, Lou Palkovics, Rex Newman, Frank Corigliano,
Al Fuchs, Bill Hagar, Larry Ciolotti, Jack Homan, Fred Spotts, Steve Nelson, Mike Helm
Third Row (l to r): Dick Johnston, Bob Sher, Ken Blanchard, Don Charles, Morris Spang, John Kothwang,
Bill Izzard, Jim Loftus, George Kuziw, Karl Isern, Marlin Berry, Joe Berarducci

Ocean City, Maryland Class Reunion

Army Signal Corps, Germany

PART TWO

REFLECTION

*I*t was August 2012, bright and sunny, and the grass and trees were incredibly green, full, and lush. I had just driven myself from my home on Cape Cod to Providence, Rhode Island, to treat myself to a leisurely Amtrak train ride to Stratford, Connecticut, to spend a weekend with my high school classmates and long-term friends.

The purpose of my trip to attend a class reunion was twofold. First, on Friday, I always looked forward to spending the evening with my two dearest friends of sixty-eight years. I usually drove to my destination and return on Saturday or Sunday.

The three of us—Carmella Matarazzo, Daniel Del Vecchio, and I—always seemed to elect to spend our first night together at a popular Italian restaurant, Roberto's, located in Monroe, Connecticut. Then on Saturday night, we got together and spent our time with a longstanding group of special friends. Our bonds had begun forming in Stoney Brook Elementary School, then continued to Wooster Junior High School and through graduation from Stratford High School.

Before I get too far ahead of myself, I want to explain that I had treated myself to this wonderful Amtrak train ride because I had not had the pleasure of enjoying such an experience for the better part of fifty years. The added benefit was to enjoy traveling the shoreline through several towns and villages that for the past fifty years, I had driven through.

I would consider myself remiss if I did not share with you at least a historical view of several of these quaint historic picturesque towns and villages. I boarded the Amtrak train in Providence, Rhode Island, with a piece of carry-on luggage and my backpack, loaded with my laptop computer and my prized possession. That prized possession was a manuscript—the manuscript for this book—in a blue plastic portfolio that I had written over the past three years. The essence of the manuscript had its beginning in what I believe was a spiritual intervention, which I described earlier. I put my carry-on on the seat beside me. I wanted to have time to review my manuscript so I would be prepared to share this story with my friends.

The train left Providence, and I was immediately enjoying the Rhode Island coastline with views of Long Island Sound. Before long—not more than an hour—we were stopping at Mystic, Connecticut, the most picturesque location of the entire ride.

Mystic itself is a quaint seaside community. Mystic Seaport is home to one of the most important collections of American maritime history. It is also the home for the *Charles W. Morgan*, the last working whaling ship and the oldest commercial vessel still in existence. This whaling ship was built in 1841 in New Bedford, Massachusetts, and sailed on thirty-seven voyages around the world spanning an eighty-year whaling career. The ship came to Mystic Seaport in 1941.

The train stopped for only a short time to pick up a few passengers. The conductor announced that the next stop would be New London. On my computer, I read that New London was founded in 1646 and had enjoyed 350 years on the Thames River. New London is the proud home of the United States Coast Guard Academy.

Once again, the train made a short stop, picking up a few more passengers, then immediately began to pick up speed after pulling out of New London's station. The conductor announced that our next stop would be Groton, Connecticut. I remembered that Groton is located on the mouth of the Housatonic River and the entryway to Long Island Sound. It is famous for its shipbuilding industry.

Before too long, the conductor announced that we would stop in New Haven and then reach my final destination, Stratford, Connecticut. About thirty-five minutes after we left New Haven, we arrived in Stratford, where I grew up, which is also located on Long Island Sound. Stratford was founded in 1639 by the Puritans. Stratford enjoys a long legacy in aviation, with helicopters being built by Sikorsky Aircraft. Avco Corporation of Stratford builds aircraft jet engines. Stratford also enjoys the legacy of the world-famous Shakespeare Theatre.

Unfortunately, the train ride seemed like it had gone too quickly, and I had been thoroughly engrossed with recalling the history and the beauty of these quaint towns and villages. As a result, I never spent much time reviewing my prized manuscript. I had placed the manuscript in the pocket of the seat in front of me, and there it had sat for the entire train ride. As the train pulled into the station, I looked out the window and saw my two friends waiting for my arrival. I was excited to see my friends again after a year and hastily reached up and pulled down my carry-on, put my backpack over my shoulder, and exited the train.

Few passengers got off the train, and it left the station quickly. The train pulled away from the station heading for New York City. My dear friends and I all hugged each other and exchanged pleasantries. We all piled into Carmella's car and headed to the Italian restaurant in Monroe. My friends expressed great interest in reading the content of my manuscript.

Sitting at a table, we ordered drinks and appetizers. We decided to delay dinner until I could share the contents of the manuscript with them. I reached into my backpack, searching every section and every pocket, and it became clear that the blue plastic portfolio containing the manuscript was not in the backpack.

I didn't want to spoil the evening, but in the back of my mind, I was worried that someone might steal my book and my ideas. I wondered what the outcome of this loss might be. Of course, I had an electronic copy, but losing the hard copy had me worried.

I did not anticipate that after the better part of a year, I would come to learn what had happened to the manuscript in the plastic portfolio.

***

Michael Barton boarded the train and settled into the seat that I had just occupied for two hours from Providence. I do not know if it was divine or spiritual intervention or just pure coincidence, but I do not question it. Michael Barton, I would later learn, is a filmmaker who was summering in Stratford with his family. He had grown up in Stratford and was commuting daily to his office in New York City. Having commuted all summer, he had nothing to do on the trip except gaze out the train window.

Because he had arrived at the station unusually late, he hadn't had the time to buy a *Wall Street Journal*. Michael Barton could have chosen to close his eyes and get some rest prior to the day's production shoot, which he anticipated lasting over the next several weeks. Instead, he thought maybe someone might have left some reading material in one of the seat pockets in front of him. He looked down and stared at a blue plastic portfolio in the seat pocket in front of him. His curiosity led him to remove the portfolio from the seat pocket and open it. It looked to him like it contained a manuscript.

Fascinated and curious about the title and about an author identified only as Cadet #271, he immediately decided how he would spend the rest of his train ride to New York City. By the time the train had pulled into Grand Central Station, Michael's insatiable appetite for reading had consumed him. He was so engrossed that the conductor, who recognized him as a daily commuter, alerted him that he should rise quickly and exit the train or he would continue on to Washington, DC. Mr. Barton exited the train with his briefcase in hand, along with the blue plastic portfolio containing the manuscript. He had already come to the conclusion that the contents of the manuscript would make an excellent movie or, at the very least, a published work.

Because this book was uniquely written with limited names attached, Michael had a major challenge. He needed to find out more about this unnamed author. He needed to know the author's identity, location, and age. He wanted to meet Cadet #271, capture the meaning of this intervention, and, lastly, find out why it was so important that the author capture his experience in print.

Michael arrived at his office anticipating a full day of production shooting for his current movie project. His desk was covered with several movie scripts and mounds of paperwork from the previous day. He placed the blue plastic portfolio on his bookcase and left the office to start his production shoot.

Several weeks later, when his vigorous schedule of production shoots was completed, he returned to his office to gather some important paperwork. His plan was to read this information over the weekend at his home in Stratford.

As he was about to leave his office, a blue aura in the corner of his eye caught his attention. Walking over to his bookcase, he thought, *Oh my God. I completely forgot to finish reading this. I never began the research.* He scooped up the blue portfolio containing the intriguing manuscript. The next day, Michael began his efforts to find the author and the answers to all of the questions that his reading had aroused.

He began with placing a telephone call to the Alumni Office at Widener University in Chester, Pennsylvania, as it had been had been Pennsylvania Military College until 1972. Upon speaking with someone at the Alumni Office, he explained the purpose of his call and asked several questions. He was successful in finding out that the author had graduated in June 1962 and currently resided in Mashpee, Massachusetts.

In anticipation of picking up the phone, making contact with Cadet #271, and introducing himself, he surprisingly found himself anxious; his hands were even moist. He dialed the telephone number.

***

When Michael called, I answered the phone.

It seemed like several moments of silence went by, and then with some trepidation, Michael replied, "Good morning. Do I have the pleasure of talking to Cadet #271, who attended Pennsylvania Military College and graduated in June of 1962?"

I quickly replied in the affirmative, thinking perhaps that one of my classmates was calling. Michael awkwardly introduced himself and explained the purpose of his telephone call. He continued by mentioning that he also had grown up in Stratford. He noted that he worked out of New York City and commuted by train to Connecticut in the summer. He continued with the introduction by saying that he was a filmmaker.

Michael took a deep breath and started by saying that several weeks before, he had boarded the train in Stratford and settled into his seat for the hour-and-a-half daily commute to New York City. Then he explained how he had come to discover the manuscript in the blue portfolio.

I anxiously interrupted and explained that in my haste to meet friends, I had forgotten to retrieve the manuscript from the seat pocket.

Michael said the manuscript was thought-provoking and compelling and had piqued his curiosity. He said that he had waited awhile to see if anyone previously sitting in this seat had neglected to take the portfolio when changing seats or exiting the train. After fifteen minutes or so, he said he had come to the conclusion that nobody was going to return, so he had taken the portfolio out of the seat pocket and begun to read the manuscript. He told me that during that hour-and-a-half train ride, he had become engaged with the contents and with the possibility of bringing this story to the screen.

Michael finally asked me if I would consider making some time for him to travel to Cape Cod to broaden his view on this wonderful story. I responded positively. Michael then offered an interesting observation about my writing. He said that I had done a wonderful job of capturing the stories and journeys of several of my high school, private school, and college classmates but had not written about my own life path.

Michael asked me if it would be possible for me to go back to the beginning of my journey and describe how I had gone about putting together my own template for life. Michael Barton, the filmmaker, would now assist me in putting this story together.

Michael and I agreed to meet at the Flying Bridge Restaurant overlooking the Falmouth Harbor Marina.

***

When I arrived at the restaurant, Michael was already seated at a table next to large windows overlooking the Marina. For some unexplainable reason, we both seemed to recognize each other. I sat down at the table, and we exchanged pleasantries. Michael was quick to indicate that he would not consider leaving the Cape, no matter how long it took, until he completely understand my journey and what had prompted me to write the manuscript.

He did not waste any time getting started. He was particularly intrigued with the introspection that said any journey can be said to have a beginning, and more times than not, an ending. He then asked me where I thought my journey had begun. I paused for a moment, took a deep breath, and said, "Michael, do you really want to know"?

He responded quickly by saying, "Yes, I really want to know, and I do not care how long it takes for you to make me understand the depth and breadth of your journey." I took a minute and then replied that I felt my personal journey started at birth. He said that was fantastic, and he also concluded that was an excellent and appropriate starting point.

And so, Michael Barton and I, Cadet #271, two complete strangers, would become closely connected in friendship and professional collaboration.

WELCOME TO THE WORLD

*M*y mother wrote in my baby book:

> *Date of Birth: October 7, 1939*
> *Height: 19 ½ inches*
> *Weight: 6lbs, 4ozs*
> *Eyes: Deep brown*
> *Hair: Reddish brown*
> *Place of Birth: Bridgeport Hospital*
> *Bridgeport, Connecticut*

1939 was also the birth year of Tina Turner, Marvin Gaye, Roberta Flack, Ralph Lauren, Mike Ditka, Neil Sedaka, Lee Majors, Dusty Springfield, and Dion Di Mucci (better known as the lead singer of Deon and the Belmonts).

The popular films included *Gone with the Wind, The Wizard of Oz, Of Mice and Men,* and *The Hunchback of Notre Dame.*

Major social events of 1939 included the opening of the New York World's Fair and of New York's LaGuardia Airport, the beginning of broadcast television and the subsequent airing of the first baseball game, and the winning of the NFL championship by Wisconsin's Green Bay Packers. Politically, Nazi Germany attacked Poland and World War II began.

New to the marketplace were nylon stockings, cellophane by DuPont Corporation, and a helicopter manufactured by Sikorsky Aircraft. The first United States food stamp program was instituted. The *Yankee Clipper* departed from New York City and landed in Southampton, England, completing the first transatlantic flight.

My first home was about four miles from downtown Bridgeport. I lived there for four years with my grandparents Franklin and Leata

Grant. They were tenants who rented the property. This three-bedroom, six-room house was located at 50 Hill Street, a side street off of North Avenue. It was built close to the railroad tracks in an industrial area. Number 50 Hill Street is a two-story house with a mansard roof and large front porch

Sometime during my four years at 50 Hill Street, my mother disappeared out of my life temporarily. I cannot remember my father ever taking an active role in my early life, and he took almost no active role at all in my later life. I came to understand that my grandfather was a special policeman and an industrial security guard. It did not take me long to figure out that my grandfather and my father were on opposite sides of the law. Dad was involved with gaming activities, not unusual for the time. My grandpa, however, was a stern man who tolerated no deviation from the law. Enough said.

Grandpa, known to all as Pat Grant, was, in my eyes, a pillar of the communities of Bridgeport and Fairfield. He was employed by Bridgeport Brass as a daytime industrial security guard, and he served as a special officer for the Bridgeport Police Department. Several nights a week, he was assigned as the officer on duty at the Ritz Ballroom. The Ritz was famous for featuring big bands such as those led by Harry James, Glen Miller, Tommy Dorsey, Lionel Hampton, and Count Basie. Grandpa was a robust man who stood tall, to me, at 5' 10". Frequently, he was mistaken as Caucasian. He was the product of an interracial marriage and had three brothers and one sister, all of whom preferred to pass for white. I was proud of my grandfather, who would have no part of that denial. His identification with the colored community did cause friction with his siblings, however.

Leata Dunbar Grant, my grandmother, grew up with her three sisters in New Milford, Connecticut. She, too, was the product of an interracial marriage, a mix of English, Irish, Native, and African descent. My maternal great-grandparents were ahead of their time, since their union occurred in the early 1880s. Grandma was short in stature but big in heart. She was a smooth-skinned, beautiful woman with Native American facial features. There are very few times I can remember when her hair was not tied in long braids. Only on special occasions did she change her braided hairstyle.

When, having been commissioned into the Army, I was leaving for Germany for three years, Grandma was not feeling well. She told me she only wanted to live until I returned home. While I was stationed in Germany, she grew gravely ill. She passed away a few months after my return home.

My mother, Elaine, was, to me, a woman of many faces: biological mother, part-time parent, friend, and stranger. The different faces seemed to appear along a continuum as I aged. As I got older, I began to understand the differences in the roles associated with these faces. Nonetheless, I did call her Mom or Ma. Physically, my mother was built like my grandfather, yet her face bore the features of both her parents. My mother was very light in complexion. Her hair was reddish-brown and not at all coarse. Her Irish descent seemed to have manifested itself in this crowning glory.

My father, Louis Robert Horner, was raised in New Haven, Connecticut. His childhood habit of kicking cans caused a lifelong moniker: His nickname, "Tin Can," or "Tinny," became his signature. He was a handsome man who was very respectful of others, especially women. In fact, he cared for his mother in his home until she was ninety years old. At that point, Tin Can arranged for her to live in a nearby nursing home. He visited her at least once a week.

Dad was a fastidious dresser with well-tailored suits and a fedora hat. He preferred late-model sedans and maintained his car to look like new. He never completed high school but became a successful businessman in the black community. He maintained friendships with several New Haven city officials. As owner of the Golden Gate nightclub, he also became friends with well-known performers of the day, including the Ink Spots (who sang "If I Didn't Care") and the Rhoda Scott Quartet. He was good friends with Charley Sifford, who helped desegregate the PGA. At my father's funeral, the widow of one of the Ink Spots shook my hand and said, "Tin Can never met a stranger."

When I was just a toddler, Mom met a Navy man stationed in New Orleans, Louisiana. For years, my belief was that my mother would pack me up and take me with her to live in New Orleans. This childhood dream never did materialize.

My grandparents strongly objected to the instability of a military life and any uncertainty of direction. Working through this as an adult, I came to understand that some sort of agreement had been reached between my grandparents, mom, and dad. I was to stay with my grandparents until my mother's life offered stability; the stability my grandparents sought for my childhood could not, in their eyes, be offered to me by my mom. Mom—God bless her—gave birth to six other children and lived in Jamaica, Queens, New York.

While I lived with Grandma and Grandpa, two other family members did show me love and give me direction. Grandma Ella, my father's mother, went to great effort to maintain ties with me. Ella Horner was a short woman and very religious. She was an active member of her church until she died in her nineties. She would often visit on Sundays and holidays. After church, she would take the train from New Haven to Bridgeport. In Bridgeport, she would board a bus to Stratford. After visiting with me for a couple of hours, she would make this same trip in reverse. Her total commute time was probably four hours. She always left in time to get home before dark.

Uncle Larry, Mom's younger brother, assumed the role of my surrogate father. I loved him long before I really knew much about my biological dad. I have no way of knowing what my life would have been like without Uncle Larry. I do know, however, that it would not have been as good.

My first memory of Uncle Larry was when he returned from the Philippines at the end of World War II. He served in an Army construction battalion building airfields and such. Like my grandfather, Uncle Larry was a teacher of values. He modeled the true meaning of friendship and respect for others. I remember an incident when my baseball team lost an important game because of several errors by others on the team. I lashed out at these teammates for their mistakes. My uncle stopped me right in the middle of my diatribe with a stern reprimand. He told me that I was not bigger than the team, that everyone had value, and that all the teammates got us to the championship game. As I recall, I looked at my uncle, who looked somewhat like Al Pacino, and said, "I'm sorry; you're absolutely right. I will never do this again." Larry died more than twenty years ago. I miss him to this day.

Holidays became associated with unsettling emotional trauma. Individuals barely more than strangers to me would sometimes arrive on separate days and announced their connections to me: "I'm your mommy" or "I'm your daddy." At a young age, it caused a lot of emotional stress to get my head around these relationships.

My father was pretty much nonexistent in my life until I was in high school and making a name for myself in sports. He sometimes attended my high school basketball games without me ever knowing he was in the stands. I do not remember my father ever attending a Little League, high school, or college baseball game. He fathered five children in addition to me. My conclusion is that he knew how to father children but did not spend any time learning how to be a parent.

My mother was not able to attend any of my athletic events. I always excused her lack of attendance by thinking she lived in Long Island and had her hands full with six children—my brothers and sisters. Since I was her firstborn, I felt strongly that my mother loved me in her own way from a distance. During the few occasions that I would spend time and talk with her, I always had the feeling that she left words unspoken. She never talked about her feelings and my abandonment. I felt my mother was one sentence away from saying, "I am sorry I left you behind."

I guess I just never got to really know my mother and father. I realize now that I never spent any time with them together under the same roof. We never shared a family meal or even a family laugh. I do know it was very difficult to experience embarrassment while I attended Elementary school. I could not complete simple paperwork at school. Questions about my mother's and father's middle names, dates of birth, street addresses, work experiences, and educational levels always came up. My teachers would just stare at me and say, "How come you do not know anything about your parents?" I had no answer. I felt small and ashamed.

Pony ride at age 5

A young soldier, age 3

Wearing my High School Sweater age 15

Wedding, 1962, with Grandparents

Wedding photo with Mom and Dad

Pat Grant on a detail

Pat Grant in police uniform

THE NEIGHBORHOOD

*W*hen I was at the ripe old age of five years old, for whatever reason—probably economic—my grandparents and I relocated from Bridgeport to a public housing project called Stoney Brook Gardens in Stratford, Connecticut. The homes were duplexes and were heated by coal furnaces. The nicest feature of this four-room house was that I had my own bedroom. Unfortunately, my daily job when I got a little older was to bank the fire for the night and empty all the ashes out of the bottom of the furnace. Sometimes the embers were still red-hot. It was certainly a joy when the heating systems in all of the houses were converted to gas about ten years later.

The address of our duplex was 53 Hull Court and posed an interesting dynamic that I never thought about or realized until I got older and began to understand institutional racism. Picture this: On one side of the street lived families whose last names were Barry, Wasko, Fox, Matarazzo, and DiSalvo. All of these families were white, and their ethnic backgrounds ran the gamut of Italian, Polish, Irish, English, and Scandinavian. Conversely, on the other side of the street, where I resided, were families named Grant, Brown, Turner, Jackson, Drayton, Farrar, and Alves. This side of the street was all black. There appeared to be an invisible line of demarcation right down the middle of the street. Oddly, you could not see it, and throughout my childhood, I never did feel it. Further, if you ventured down to Underwood Court, the racial composition was all black families. Going in the opposite direction to Baird Court, Marsh Way, Singer Court, or Sikorsky Place, guess what—all the residents were white. The demographics of Stoney Brook Gardens public housing were purposeful, not accidental. This is probably not too different from other neighborhoods in the United States at the time.

All of the families and the children growing up in my block were, in my judgment, the best neighbors I could have experienced. The parents and, by extension, their children believed we were all in the same economic pot together. They behaved in such a way that each enjoyed and protected the other.

This neighborhood was clean, safe. Neighbors really cared about not only their own children but everyone else's as well. We would play games outside until it got to be dusk. All the kids knew that the streetlights going on was the signal for us to hightail it home. Woe to you if you were late! There were times when other parents in the neighborhood would grab me by the hand to escort me home. When this did happen, I could anticipate some sort of punishment or restriction, maybe both.

CHILDHOOD FRIENDS

I have briefly tried to describe the neighborhood and the environment that I grew up in. None of my childhood memories would be complete without my feelings and thoughts about my sixty-eight-year friendships years with wonderful, unvarnished men and women such as Carmella Materazzo, Daniel Del Vecchio, Ethel Barry, Mary Ann Fritzky, Cecelia Lancia, Michael Sweeney, Jim McQuillan, Ralph Alves, Rodney Turner, Milton Billy Jackson, and Roger Sullivan. I could go on with this list of childhood friends, but these are just a few who just came to mind. I do certainly apologize to anyone who is feeling left out.

When I started this journey to describe this time in my life, I thought it would be more authentic if I asked several of my childhood friends to reach back and capture some of their thoughts and feelings. I asked them to write about my friendship with them beginning with our time together in elementary school. I guess I should title the following memoirs as their stories.

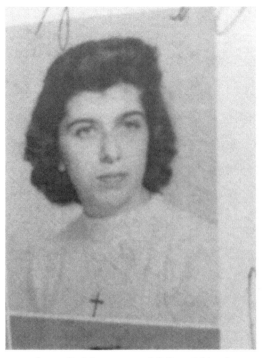

Carmella Matarazzo, childhood friend

Depending on who was speaking with her, you would hear people address her as Carmella, Carm, or Dolly. I have personally addressed Carmella Matarazzo Fawver by all three names in the same conversation. She says her prize possession is a beaded bracelet. Each bead symbolizes one of her children or grandchildren. If you look at it closely, you will see that included on the bracelet are beads that symbolize both Daniel Del Vecchio and me. I am honored.

When Carmella talks with me about our childhood, she remembers all of us playing hide-and-seek while all of our parents sat in lawn chairs, watching us. Every morning, we would walk to the school bus stop, sit on the stone wall, and wait for the bus. She was particularly fond of my grandfather because he would take a gang of eight of us to the Ritz Ballroom whenever there was a Square Dance Night. As kids, we looked forward to the all-you-can-eat free hotdogs and soda. Dolly also recalls the summer trips to Beardsley Park for swimming. As she reflected on our childhood, she summed it up by saying, "We had a fairytale neighborhood with a mix of all races, colors, and nationalities. Growing up, we did not realize the difference. All we knew is that we had great friends and had a lot of fun." Significant to me was her remark that she always felt I was destined for greatness. I do not know how she defines greatness, as it is different for everybody, but I do feel that maybe I let her down.

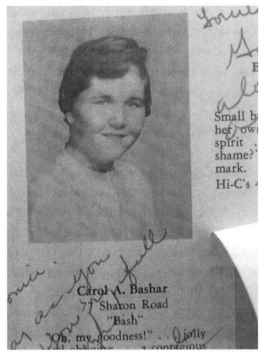

Ethel Barry, childhood friend

Ethel Marie Barry is named after her mother. Growing up, we called her Ree, shortening her middle name. We continue this today. Ree's parents raised six children and lived across the street from me. There were four boys, including a set of twins, and two girls. At present, only Ree and her youngest brother, Edward, are still living.

Ree remembers all of us neighborhood kids knocking on Mr. & Mrs. DiSalvo's door to ask, "Can we watch Howdy Doody and Clarabelle?" Their four-inch black-and-white television was the only one in the neighborhood.

Ree's stories helped me remember what good people the DiSalvos really were.

Mr. DiSalvo spoke only Italian. When he spoke to his wife, the unfamiliar words and tones sounded to us kids like he was fighting with her. Often, he would suddenly sit down on the floor and start laughing. At first we were bewildered, but after many television visits, we figured out that the DiSalvos were not fighting. We always looked forward to summer because their daughter worked in the garment district in New York City and each summer, she would bring us new bathing suits.

Mary Ann Fritzky, childhood friend

Mary Ann Fritzky Massa recently spoke to me about a fond memory of our friendship in sixth grade. At Stoney Brook School, our teacher, Miss Caruso, was just out of college. She was young and progressive for her time. During recess, we would often move all of the desks to the outer wall to have a dance party.

Looking back, it is clear that Miss Caruso was very fond of music. Mary Ann recalled that once, Miss Caruso had us perform an operetta based on the movie *The Toast of New Orleans*. This 1951 musical starred Mario Lanza and Katherine Grayson. I was the leading man, and Mary Ann was the leading lady. On stage, we stood on a tabletop while holding hands and singing "Be My Love." Mary Ann enthusiastically recalled that she and I were "pretty fantastic." I make no such claim for myself.

Mary Ann chose to share her memory of some drama that took place when it came time for a school dance. She said it was well known that I had a childhood crush on a fair-skinned Irish classmate named Julie Cuddy. I invited Julie to go to the dance with me and she really wanted to accept. Much to our disappointment, her parents spoke contemptuously of my invitation. Interracial friendships, let alone a date—even to an elementary school dance—were not going to be a part of their daughter's life.

Although I had forgotten about this a long time ago, it is just one example of events in the fifties that affected me. It no doubt contributed to how I formulated conclusions on how to deal with racism.

Mary Ann went on to say that I was always popular, as demonstrated by my election as class president for two consecutive years. "Many girls wanted to be with a great athlete, but," she said, "the times were not favorable for interracial dating."

As a footnote, many years later, at one of our class reunions, Julie and I renewed our friendship without interference from parents. Julie soon visited me, traveling from Georgia to Massachusetts. The renewed affection was intense. Sadly, our friendship was cut short by Julie's untimely passing due to cancer. Once again, it seems, this connection was not to be.

Danny Del Vecchio, childhood friend

My friend for life and the most respected man I have ever known is Daniel Del Vecchio. He is unvarnished; what you see is what you get. As boys, Danny and I were as close as two friends could be. Years later, Danny's mother remarked, "You two were always together—up to something. I even thought that you were starting to look alike." We both roared.

Our "up-to-something" list was very long. We both tried to learn to tap dance in the office shed at the baseball field. Neither Danny nor I was very successful, but we sure made that shed rock. Practice sessions were halted when Coach Burns found us pounding away on the very day we had skipped batting practice!

We both tried to make a loud whistle with no fingers through our teeth. Practicing this before class was frowned upon by our third-grade teacher, Miss Philips. Jointly, we decided not to like her.

I recall teaching Danny how a left-handed person like me wrote; he was fascinated that I held a pencil differently than he did. Danny taught me how to make model airplanes out of balsam wood.

We both liked camping and joined the Cub Scouts and Boy Scouts as a team. We would fly kites and would build forts and lean-tos out of wood without using tools or nails. One of the highlights of our childhood was going to the pig farm in the swamp and getting chased by the pigs. We always ended up in the mud, rolling around and getting just as dirty as the pigs. As young boys, Danny and I were naïve and impressionable. Since we were all covered with mud, we just knew we were both going to get sick. Danny, more than I, was emphatic that we would catch polio. We thought that this was the worst thing that could happen.

By the age of fourteen, Danny and I started taking the ten-mile bus ride to Bridgeport to Stevens Men's Shop to buy shirts and other manly accessories. In later years when we talked about this experience, we concluded we must have looked pretty silly standing in the middle of the store, wearing dungarees and short-sleeved plaid shirts while the salesman held a narrow blue-striped tie, demonstrating how to tie a Windsor knot. Danny still has the card with the directions after fifty-five years. I mastered the Windsor knot many times over during my stint in corporate America. I have tossed out the directions along with several dozen ties.

We continued our close friendship throughout junior high and high school. From our freshman year on, I got involved in basketball and baseball while Danny busied himself with clubs. We did not grow apart in high school, however. In fact, during my two-year tenure as class president, Danny served as the class treasurer. Dolly first referred to us as the "bookends"; other classmates took up the term as a short-cut two-syllable moniker for Louie and Danny. Today I cringe when called Louie and much prefer Louis. Old classmates are given a pass on this offense, however.

Our friendship continues strengthening even to this day. After reading portions of my manuscript, Danny shared with me that he reads the daily obituaries. He looks for death notices of veterans and has come to wondering if these veterans have families left behind. "I wonder," Danny choked with emotion, "who will water their flowers? More vets from World War Two, Korea, and Vietnam are passing away. I wonder who will be left who remembers them." I am a better man because of Danny's friendship.

As already stated, I was not the only black or multiracial kid on the block. I had many persons of color among my boyhood friends. Still alive are Michael Turner, Terry Griffin, Larry Lazaro, Teddy Robinson, Billy Jackson and his brother Milton, and Ron Davis. This past August, I received an e-mail from Ron. I hadn't heard from him in five decades.

Ron graduated in 1959 from Harding High School in Bridgeport. Presently, he is the track coach at San Jose State University. In 1959, he set a state record in the mile run; his time was the sixth fastest clocking in the country. Ron and his family would come to visit relatives in the neighborhood where I lived. We played together and became friends during these visits. Ron had spotted me on Facebook and decided to e-mail me. I was honored when he wrote that he had been inspired by my accomplishments in high school sports.

When I caught up on his history and read about his accomplishments in sports and his career in track and field, my admiration for Ron only grew. Ron has coached Ohio State, Maryland Eastern Shores, South Alabama, and San Jose State. Additionally, he has trained athletes the world over, helping them win Olympic medals. I am so proud of him. You never know as a kid where life may lead you or your friends.

***

Glancing at my watch, I said, "It feels like I have been talking for hours."

Michael Barton, demonstrating a dry sense of humor, replied, "You have." Leaning back in his seat, he then smiled and gestured that I should continue.

STRATFORD LITTLE LEAGUE

*L*ittle League Baseball commenced in the Town of Stratford in 1949. Two Stratford residents, Sy Knepler and Vincent Devitto, made inquiries about this rapidly growing program, which had originated in Williamsport, Pennsylvania. Knepler and Devitto met with Bernard O' Rourke, the Connecticut Little League Commissioner. They learned of a proposed baseball league for boys between the ages of eight and twelve. Convinced of the value of the program, they endorsed it in its entirety.

Their first task was to secure a financial sponsor for the required four-team league. The Raybestos Company, which manufactures automobile brake lining, signed on to sponsor the Stratford Little League. They made Raybestos Memorial Field the playing site for all league games. The four teams were formed: Holy Name, Sterling House, Lordship, and Raybestos.

During 1949 and1950, there were no boys of color playing in the Stratford league. Somehow, I found my way to John Dolyak, the manager of the Holy Name team through my friendship with Steve Royal.

I went to elementary school with Steve, and he was already playing for Holy Name. He and I played ball together at Stoney Brook School. Steve is Catholic and attended Holy Name Church during those years, so during the summer, he played on the Holy Name team. One day, he invited me to go to practice with him; it was then that I met Coach Dolyak. Coach gave me a tryout, and that is how my whole baseball life began. Thanks, Steve.

At that young age, although I did not know the word racism, I did feel excluded. The other kids were white and I was black. I was told I could not play. "Go home," they said. I felt like the Jackie Robinson of the Stratford Little League. All I wanted to do was play baseball.

I can recall vividly Coach Dolyak saying, "Louie, get ready to go to the field, but don't put on your uniform." I did not understand, but I did what he asked. I got in one of the cars, the only kid carrying, not wearing, a uniform. At the ball field, I could see my coach meeting with other coaches and officials. I can remember, as if it were yesterday, Coach Dolyak waving his arms and shouting to this group of grown men, "If Louie can't play, then the Holy Name team is not playing."

Coach Dolyak probably felt like the Branch Rickey of Stratford Little League. After much commotion and shouting back and forth, he succeeded in breaking the color barrier. On that day, he brought racism to its knees. Ironically, in 1951, I led the league in batting percentage. The following year, our team won the league championship. I was never again told, "Don't put on your uniform."

On a lighter note, I was not only the only boy of color on the Holy Name team but was also the only Episcopalian. Father Filip took care of that. He came to me one day at practice and asked, "Louie, did you ever think about converting?"

I quivered. "I'm sorry, Father; I don't know what you mean." With that, my road to conversion began. I remain a Catholic to this day.

THOSE WERE THE DAYS

CONTRIBUTED PHOTO

It's been 60 years since Holy Name Church won the 1952 Stratford Original Little League championship. Front row, from left: Bob Vena, Bob Dolyak, Lou Horner, Dan Ricco, Fran Cholko and John Pappa. Second row: Bob Babjak, John Chickos, George Dube, Dan Guerra, Dave Karponai, George Poremba, Larry Dzubin, Steve Thrush and Mike Martin. Third row: coach Sal Cholko, Holy Name Pastor Rev. John Filip and manager John Dolyak. Horner and Pappa were the top pitchers; Guerra and Dolyak the top hitters (both over .600) and Cholko the home run leader. Pappa went on to pitch in the majors with the Baltimore Orioles. The Stratford Original All-Stars finished second in the state tournament to Stamford, which went on to win the Little League World Series.

Little League

Little League Banquet

On our way to Ebberts Field

Focusing on the job

Heading to our TV appearance

On TV: Happy Felton's Knot Hole Gang, Brooklyn, NY

STRATFORD HIGH SCHOOL

I entered Stratford High School for my sophomore year in the 1954–1955 academic year after spending my ninth-grade academic year at Wooster Junior High School and enjoyed the distinction of being part of the first class to ever graduate from this new school. I did not have any idea what the high school environment was going to entail. My main focuses were going to be academics, sports, and clubs and activities, in that order. Several of my friends and classmates suggested and offered support for my running for class president. I was honored that my classmates were providing their support. I gave it some thought and concluded that I would seek the presidency.

I suddenly realized that in addition to Wooster Junior High students coming to the high school, we would be joined by students who had spent ninth grade at Johnson Junior High School, located at the other end of the town. The broader complexity I was faced with in running for election was the fact that my main goal was to bring together students from all multicultural, social, racial and ethnic backgrounds, so the main focus of my campaign platform was to stress that we were going to spend three years together and it was my desire and goal that we have fun, work hard, and graduate as the Class of 1957. My approach worked.

The following week, an article appeared in the local newspaper, the *Bridgeport Post*, which started off by saying that if the leaders of the anti-Negro attacks in Milford, Delaware, wanted to see democracy in action, they should have dropped by Stratford High School that week. The article explained that their readers would have seen a fifteen-year-old colored boy elected president of the sophomore class. (I overwhelmingly won the election, garnering 300 votes out of the 400 cast.) The article went on to highlight that I had selected a Jewish girl, Susan Koskoff, to be my campaign manager. Together, our appeal for unity had won the hearts and minds of our classmates. Not too surprisingly, the junior class presidential election was a carbon copy of the first; I just secured more votes.

I stated earlier that I wanted to focus on three areas in high school, which included academics, sports, and clubs and activities. Being elected to the presidency in my sophomore and junior years led me to increase participation in clubs and activities. In my attempt to focus on my academics, it appeared that my grades reflected that I was just about a middle-of-the-road student. Sometimes I would excel in one of my subjects, and other times, I would experience difficulty in some of my subjects. I lacked direction and did not ask for assistance or know where to go to get it. I blame no one but myself. In the last semester of my junior year, I experienced some academic difficulty with chemistry. I cannot remember if I was the problem or if I just could not get my arms around that teacher's method of communicating. Maybe I had just never developed good study habits. My homeroom teacher, Mrs. Ohla, approached this teacher on my behalf and explained that I was more than willing to do extra work to bring up my grade. The teacher declined. In front of the whole class he even said that the only thing good that I was going to do in life was to bounce basketballs.

I could still participate in sports, but his declination meant that I was not able to seek the office of senior class president. I was devastated. I had let my friends and classmates down.

What still amazes me to this day is that after all these years, many of my classmates still refer to me as their only true class president..

The last focus in high school for me was sports. I had primed myself for this stage since participating in Little League baseball. In my three years of playing baseball, I was elected to the all-district team and was elected captain of our team. Not Bad.

Class President (me) and his staff

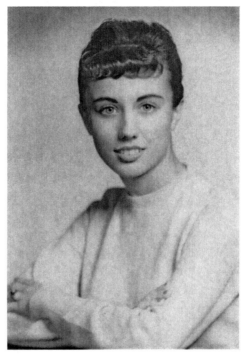

Julia Cuddy, my first girlfriend

High school singing group, The Echoes

Stratford High School Graduation photo, 1957

The team captain at play

Danny Del Vecchio, my boyhood friend, and I.

Mary Ann Fritzky and Carmella Matarazzo

Classmates at High School Reunion

Michael Sweeney (right) and Louis Horner

Ethel Barry, my neighborhood friend, and I

The 3 Amigos: Louis, Carmella, Danny

Stoney Brook/Stratford High School Reunion

PEEKSKILL MILITARY ACADEMY

*I*n 1957, after graduating from Stratford, I alone came to the conclusion that I was not sufficiently prepared to attend college right away. The athletic part of my soul was intact, but the emotional and intellectual parts of my soul were, at best, splintered. I had gone through my senior year in high school concerned about my reading comprehension and my middle-of-the-road passing grades. I was still feeling the effects of letting my friends and classmates down for being academically ineligible to secure the position as senior class president.

In my senior year, I did visit several colleges and universities, such as Holy Cross, Clarke, Colby, the University of Connecticut, and the University of Hartford. Truthfully, I was more focused on the possibility of playing sports for one of these institutions than on their academic reputations. The expectations of my grandparents, uncle, and others weighed on me. I felt the pressure of being the first family member to graduate from high school, let alone college! I do not today find fault, but, with the exception of my uncle's help, I was pretty much on my own when it came to deciding about college. I never received any information or assistance from my parents, grandparents, coaches, or friends. As a result, I felt like I was playing with half a deck of cards when I visited these campuses.

My appreciation goes out to Uncle Larry, my mother's brother, who would take the time out of work to drive me to any of the colleges or universities of my choosing. He supported me emotionally during this time just as he had when I was a little boy playing ball.

In the summer of 1957, I enrolled in a reading-comprehension course at the University of Bridgeport. The course opened my eyes to the importance of reading and the proper approach to academic studies.

During that summer, my grandparents and I were contacted by a man associated with athletics at the United States Military Academy at West Point. (I wish I could remember who he was, but I don't.) In a short time, Uncle Larry was once again driving me to a campus visit. This time it was West Point.

This visit was my first introduction to a true military environment and to the importance placed on graduating as a commissioned officer. Inspired, I realized this accomplishment was right up there beside my desire for athletic accomplishment. The whole environment was attractive and stimulating. Unfortunately for me, the timing was not right. All appointments to the freshman class were filled. I was advised that appointments to West Point were also somewhat political. Through subsequent discussions with admissions officers, I agreed upon a decided approach.

The plan was that I attend Peekskill Military Academy for one year as a postgraduate student to prepare for an appointment to West Point. Now I came upon a mountain to climb. I was going to have the proud distinction of being the first African American student to attend Peekskill Military Academy (PMA) in its 135 years of existence.

In 1833, PMA had been founded in Peekskill, New York. It was built beside a tree where a Revolutionary War British spy had been hanged. At one time, PMA was one of the largest preparatory schools in America. Since its founding, the school had physically and intellectually challenged young men from forty-two states and twenty-seven countries.

The Vietnam War would trigger an unprecedented antimilitary attitude throughout the United States. Almost overnight, the public perception of all things military would turn from pride and encouragement to distaste and disdain. School officials would decide to close the academy after the graduation of the Class of 1968. Eleven years prior to its closing, I made my unceremonious entrance into PMA, intending to use a year to prepare for four years up the river at West Point.

The military environment was strict and regimented. It was an eyeopener, in a positive way. My interests in academics and sports were right up there with my new passion for a possible career in the military.

I cannot say enough about my three closest friendships that materialized during my yearlong stay at Peekskill. My roommate was a boy named Vincent Armetta from Brooklyn who volunteered to room with me. I do think he was handpicked, since finding a roommate for a non-white cadet was considered an administrative challenge. Vincent's career would bear similarities to mine. He worked for IBM, and I for Digital Equipment. We remained friends long after we graduated from PMA. Sadly, Vinnie passed away in mid-life from complications due to diabetes. Diane, his widow, and I still keep in touch.

My second friend from PMA was a boy named Steve Brietbart whose home was Longmeadow, Massachusetts. We immediately developed a great relationship and are still the best of friends today. He currently resides with his wife in the suburbs of Atlanta, Georgia.

The last of my three closest friends at PMA was a boy named Edward De Sevo, who lived in Jersey City, New Jersey. Of all my friends, I found Edward to be the most introspective about life, people, and friendships. On May 6, 1958, he gave me an 8" x 10" photograph of himself because he wanted to express his feelings about our friendship and he needed the space to write his thoughts.

On the back of the photo Edward wrote the following: "Between you, Vincent and I, I can't picture a better bunch of buddies." He wrote, "You are tops in my book and always will be. We had some rough times this year but by watching you and following your example, I learned to become a man. I am proud to say I am your buddy." He went on to declare that he would never forget my smile and my wonderful kindness. He felt I would leave PMA and someday be a great success in the eyes of my parents, grandparents, and friends. Finally, he closed with writing that he was not saying good-bye, but just saying hello to a never-ending friendship.

After all of this, I thought I could add no further thoughts about what my friends meant to me over the course of that one year at Peekskill. Then I started reading through my PMA yearbook and came to the picture of my company commander, Raul Martinez, from Santurce, Puerto Rico.

Looking at Raul's picture brought fond memories of my year at PMA. With a great sense of humility, I proceeded to read what Raul had written in my yearbook: "Although we were together only one year, I found you to be more than just a friend. I enjoyed having you in my Company because you did what I could never do ... not only raising the morale in my company, but in the whole school. Never let anyone take that greatness from you."

I cannot end discussion of my PMA experience without talking about another part of my being: my athletic experiences in that one year. I was fortunate enough to play basketball and baseball. The highlight of my short career in basketball there was during a game with a school named Lake Grove. We rolled up a victory of 110–42. In this game, I scored fifty-seven points, setting a new county record. To my knowledge, this record has never been matched or broken. Our team that year added two more names to the list of the greatest basketball players to have played at PMC: Francis Quinn and Louis F. Horner.

Graduation time quickly approached, and I strongly believed I wanted to pursue a military career. I realized that attending West Point was not for me, as I was not ready to commit to four years of military service. I began to explore alternatives with the assistance of the guidance counselor. At the time, there were four possible military institutions I could consider attending.

In 1958, I quickly decided to rule out the Citadel, located in Charleston, South Carolina, and Virginia Military Institute, located in Lexington, Virginia. I assure you, Uncle Larry agreed with me. "Don't go south," he cautioned me. I also decided against Norwich University, in Vermont, which seemed like it was planets away and had unfavorable weather conditions. That took me down to one final choice: Pennsylvania Military College, located in Chester, Pennsylvania.

If I was going to pursue a military institution, the decision to attend PMC was a fortuitous one. It seems as if I had an angel looking over me. I strongly believe I was directed to the greatest collection of men, classmates, friends, and brothers for life. And so my journey through life continued with many paths and challenges looming ahead.

Louis Horner, 1958

Edward DeSevo, PMA buddy

Vincent Armetta, Peekskill room mate and best friend

Steve Breitbart, PMA buddy

Raul Martinez, PMA friend

THE CORPORATE JOURNEY

*I*n October 1965, I returned to the United States after spending three years in the Army, 26th Signal Corps, in Ludwigsburg, Germany. My aspirations of pursuing a military career were significantly dimmed when I experienced how the real Army operated. After spending one year at PMA and four years at PMC, I had developed regimentation, organization, honor, and integrity All of these things had been continually woven into my moral fabric. I am sorry to say I saw very few of these attributes demonstrated by superior officers during my stint in the Army, so, painfully, I elected to end my military career and pursue a corporate journey.

As I look back at investing forty years of my life in the corporate environment, I see my biggest mistake was that I believed in people who, ultimately, did not believe in me. It did not matter whether these people were below me or above me in the hierarchy. Trust, faith, honesty, and friendship did at times betray and disappoint me. Many times, I found myself grasping to understand why my loyalty was not reciprocated.

My first introduction into corporate America was as a sales correspondent in the International Marketing Department of Homelite, a division of Textron Corporation, which was located in Byram, Connecticut. Homelite is a manufacturer of chainsaws, pumps, and generators. Three other sales correspondents and I, along with a manager, were responsible for developing and opening new distributorships for the brand. I loved this job and got to correspond with and develop great friendships with people from all over the world. On the downside, I lived approximately sixty miles from this job; after three years, the distance became physically and financially draining and I began to seek other employment.

I was contacted by an employee relations manager at Avco Lycoming Corporation located in Stratford, Connecticut, where I was presently living. He had followed my athletic career throughout high school and wanted to know if I would be interested in working and playing baseball for Avco. I was flattered but wanted to know why this would be a good career move. I didn't expect to earn a living playing ball. The ER manager was ready with his persuasive arguments: more money, shorter commute, travel while playing ball, career opportunities of a larger corporation, and job opportunities for my then wife. I was hired by Avco Corporation, manufacturer of jet engines, into the Records Retentions Department.

The vice president of Human Resources had received good reports about my work record and set up a meeting with me at his office. He asked me if I had ever thought about a career in human resources. I immediately replied that I had, and I jumped at the opportunity. My human resources career began.

My first HR job was interviewing and recruiting nonexempt employees. Over the next two years, I acquired experience in exempt, college, and technical recruiting. Human resources was becoming part of who I was; however, there were other components of human resources that I needed to learn, and I set out to get this work experience.

I interviewed with Burndy Corporation, a manufacturer of electrical connectors and terminals, located in Norwalk, Connecticut. I was hired as a Human Resources manager of administration, with involvement in the areas of compensation, benefits, affirmative action, and policies and procedures.

At Burndy, I developed a good friendship with an African American engineer named Leroy Saylor. In 1970, I was responsible for conducting Leroy's exit interview. He indicated that he had accepted and offered a position with Digital Equipment Corporation located in Maynard, Massachusetts. Interestingly enough, Digital had been founded in 1957 and only hired its second African American exempt employee after thirteen years. This employee was Leroy.

During the exit interview, Leroy expressed a desire to start an inner-city manufacturing facility somewhere in Massachusetts. "When I do," he said, "I will call you. Maybe you will be interested in the Human Resource manager's position." Four years later, Leroy kept his promise. On this occasion, my faith in someone was rewarded. Leroy called me to say he had written a business plan. He wanted me to meet him at the Springfield Armory in Springfield, Massachusetts. As a result of this meeting, I began my twenty-year career at Digital Equipment Corporation.

During the four years after Leroy left Burndy, I felt I needed more comprehensive knowledge and experience in the areas of compensation and benefits. I was recruited by Berol Corporation, the manufacturer of writing instruments and pencil sharpeners, located in Danbury, Connecticut. I was hired as the Benefits and Compensation manager at their corporate headquarters. During the four years that I worked there, I was never really was comfortable with the environment, being the first African American to work at their corporate headquarters. Although the corporate headquarters employed only approximately fifty employees, my instincts to move on from Berol were to serve me well.

In 1974, after Leroy called, I joined Digital Equipment Corporation as the Human Resource manager of the Springfield manufacturing facility. The plant was responsible for manufacturing module boards, power supplies, cables, and harnesses. Our charter included a goal of 50 percent people of color in management and nonexempt employees. We achieved that goal. Nonetheless, our biggest challenge in achieving the goal was to change mind-sets, behaviors, and work ethics of our entirely new workforce.

Making sure employees understood how important their contribution was to the overall manufacturing goal was tantamount to me. I am proud to say the Springfield manufacturing facility grew from 0 to 850 employees in three and a half years; it became one of the most successful minority manufacturing plants in the world. If you consider transfer cost as a criterion and superimpose a selling price that includes labor, overhead, and material, then the facility approached 2 billion dollars in sales.

This success led to Leroy being asked to establish a similar plant start-up in Boston. He accepted, and reluctantly, I declined the opportunity to assist him. Instead, I accepted a position as Compensation manager for Volume Manufacturing. After a year, the vice president of Human Resources for Manufacturing developed a new concept to measure the Human Resources organization as a business in support of business partners. He asked me to head up this effort as the Human Resources business manager. Through collaborative efforts, we were able to measure according to business metrics the Human Resources impact on the individual businesses. We, as an organization, were pleasantly surprised at the results.

I was subsequently promoted to the position of group Human Resources manager of Technical Group Marketing and three years later promoted again, to the position of group Human Resources manager of Computer Systems Manufacturing. It was now 1990, and the human resources world was changing, as was Digital Equipment's role and position in the computer industry. I concluded that it was time to make a decision to go in one of two directions. I could seek employment at another corporation or I could start my own business within Digital. My thoughts were to consider a business group not directly aligned with the everyday activities of Human Resources.

I wrote a business plan to gather a small cadre of Digital employees and launch the Strategic Alliances and Initiatives Group. Our charter and goals included making interventions into historical black colleges and universities to teach professors, students, and small local businesses the value of technology such as CAD/CAM, animation, solid modeling, and stereolithography. I read about the superb efforts of Father William Cunningham, a Catholic priest, who was trying to open a manufacturing facility in the heart of Detroit, Michigan. Without introduction, I called him and explained to him that I felt Digital Equipment Corporation and my start-up group could assist him in achieving his goals. The rest is history. We were instrumental in helping him open a manufacturing facility fabricating parts for Roger Penske. As part of our effort in Michigan, we were also instrumental in the development of an associate degree program for manufacturing at Michigan State.

digital
MAYNARD
DIGITAL THIS WEEK

Volume 12, Number 18

October 7, 1985

Digital receives Presidential Citation award for computer camp program

Digital is the recent recipient of an award from the President's Citation Program for Private Sector Initiatives for the company's support of Project 50/50: The Computer Program. The award was presented by President Ronald Reagan to Lou Horner, Group Personnel manager, Computer Systems Manufacturing, at a ceremony on the South Lawn of the Executive Mansion.

Project 50/50 is a regional computer-based education program developed by Lou Horner, who secured joint sponsorship from Digital, the French River Education Center and the Oxford, Massachusetts, Public Schools. Now in its third year, the program has been nationally validated by the U.S. Department of Education's Joint Dissemination Review Panel, and is a National Diffusion Network program that has been designated as a model for adoption or adaption by other schools.

Al Mullin, vice president, Corporate Relations, said, "While Digital is honored to be recognized for its sponsorship of the Project 50/50 Computer Camp Program, the efforts of Lou Horner, the French River Education Center, and the Oxford, Massachusetts, Public Schools really make the program as successful as it is. Without their dedication and coordinating efforts among the participating school districts, the Project would not have come to fruition."

Through Project 50/50, 74 teachers and more than 1,000 students, half of whom were ethnic minority, female and/or economically disadvantaged, have been enrolled in courses in programming, computer science, electronics and career awareness. The program covers 20 school districts, including Auburn, Charleton, Dudley, Framingham, Leicester, Marlboro, Northboro, Oxford, Southboro, Southbridge, Sturbridge, Webster, and Worcester, Massachusetts. From New Hampshire, participating schools include Amherst, Derry, Hudson, Littleton, Merrimack, Milford, and Nashua.

Funding and computer equipment for Project 50/50 are provided through Digital's Corporate Contributions Program, of which a major objective is to increase computer literacy and the use of computers as educational tools, and to broaden the access of women and minorities to careers within the computer industry.

The President's Citation Program for Pri-

(l-r)Ken Olsen, president, and Lou Horner, Group Personnel manager, Computer Systems Manufacturing, hold the Presidential Citation award given to Digital in support of the Project 50/50 computer camp program. Lou, who developed Project 50/50, recently received the award from President Ronald Reagan at a ceremony held at the White House in Washington, D.C.

vate Sector Initiatives was developed to encourage the growth in voluntary service programs on the part of businesses, trade associations, and professional societies by recognizing the outstanding contributions that are already being made. Private sector initiatives include volunteerism, corporate social responsibility, public-private partnerships, philanthropy, and privitization programs. ■

Digital ships 75th VAX-11/780 in $39-million contract with General Electric

Digital has announced the shipment of its 75th VAX-11/780 computer system to General Electric Company's Simulation and Control Systems Department, Daytona Beach, Florida.

The shipment is part of a five-year contract, estimated at $39 million, to provide GE with 270 VAX-11/780 computers for tank simulator systems created by GE specifically for the U.S. Army.

The VAX systems, VMS software, disk drives and associated peripherals are being supplied and serviced by Digital's Government Systems Group, Merrimack, N.H. The systems will be incorporated into the COFT (Conduct of Fire Trainer) tank simulator system.

According to GE, the COFT mobile tank-crew training stations will be installed in military facilities in the U.S., West Germany and Korea. The COFT system circumvents the costs (fuel and ammunition), dangers, and difficulties of producing combat-like conditions for training.

The computerized system reproduces the appearance and functions of a modern tank's interior controls, indicators, and weapons systems. It also produces full-color, computer-generated action scenes that represent the view from a real tank including target motion, enemy artillery/tank fire, and variable weather conditions.

The system is controlled by a VAX-11/780 system that interfaces with the crew compartment, calculates complex ballistic equations, monitors the tank crew's responses, and performs training management functions, including recommendations of additional exercises. ■

Announcing the Computer Camp Award

The staff of the yearbook of the class of 1985 would like to
dedicate this to Mr. Lou Horner. Without him, there would be no
camp and no yearbook. Project 50/50 was his idea that he brought
from dream to reality. We would like to thank him for his
efforts.

Good-bye

The time has come
To say good-bye
To all our friends
Both girl and guy.

We learned about computers
We made some new friends
Our class can't be forgotten
We started a trend.

I hope it continues
For the years ahead
The enjoyment here
Is something to spread

The memories we made
Are ours forever
Thanks to this camp-
Lou Horner's endeavor.

By Debbie Travers

Camp Kids

Working at Burndy Corporation

Senator Ted Kennedy visits the Digital Springfield, MA plant

Unity Bracelet

SOCIAL AND RACIAL INDIGNITIES

*I*t seems that my birthright of a multiracial background has repeatedly exposed me to experiences that I consider to be social and racial indignities. To my way of thinking, they were a result of learned behavior, peer pressure, jealousy, competitiveness, and a desire for power and control. I think that demonstrations of superiority were really expressions of insecurity. In any case, we all arrive on this earth without these attributes and negative behaviors. I cannot remember requesting to be treated unfairly or exposed to injustices, yet repeatedly, I was treated in this manner.

Over the years, I have engaged in many conversations with people of color with respect to their thoughts and feelings on these matters. I heard many common themes, such as needing to perform better to be equal, being made to feel that you are less than those who are considered white, being followed around in stores, and noticing women clutch their handbags whenever you enter an elevator. These recurring experiences, though subtle, cause a person to acquire a heightened sense of awareness. I know I began to anticipate potential situations.

When attending corporate functions, I would excuse myself and leave after a short time. Early in my career, I found that alcohol can give rise to a sense of power both in my peers and in upper management. They would feel the need to engage me in a conversation about how I was "different from the rest" (meaning other people of color). Categorizing "the rest" was not a conversation I wanted to have with someone who had been drinking.

I consider myself very fortunate that most of my childhood, high school, and college experiences were void of discriminatory behavior. My friends and classmates were and are the best anyone could know. There is an expression about playing the cards that you are dealt. I must say that with regards to the cards I was dealt for life's journey, I feel fortunate and appreciative. I feel strongly that I am a better person because I have had good people in my life.

Further reflection has led me to conclude that from birth, we are "dealt a hand" without a label. We can compare our lives to glasses half full or glasses half empty. When we are faced with unsettling situations, we react according to our own perceptions of our cards. Many, like myself, are given daily reminders of one aspect of our cards, such as race, gender, or sexual orientation. The challenge for me has been not to allow just one aspect of my being define who I am.

With that being said, several memorable life-changing experiences confronted me. I hope the events opened not only my eyes but also those of the other persons involved.

No Compensation

It was 1970 when I accepted the position as Human Resource manager of Compensation and Benefits for Berol Corporation in Danbury, Connecticut. During my third year there, I was confronted with two racially charged social situations that I was unprepared to deal with. Ironically, both incidents took place within a short time span during the Christmas holidays.

The vice president and the director of Human Resources and me, along with three consultants from New Jersey, spent the better part of two weeks together constructing a revised pension and benefits plan package. Finally, after many discussions, the project was completed and finalized. We all gave a sigh of relief and proceeded to have lunch. Fifteen minutes earlier, coffee and sandwiches had been delivered to the conference room, and we were eager to dig in. As we were eating, each participant recounted some of the difficulties and complications of the multifaceted plan; we told what we called corporate war stories. During this banter, the vice president of HR blurted out, "Jesus Christ, this project was as complicated as looking for a nigger in a woodpile."

The room went silent. I closed my notebook, picked up my papers, and moved toward the door, saying, "Good afternoon, gentlemen." I closed the door firmly behind me.

The VP came bounding out the door, expressing his apologies. He explained that he was tired and not thinking clearly. Unclear thinking was not a luxury I could afford. Once again, I had to gather my thoughts and quickly regain my composure. After pausing, I looked him straight in the eyes and said, "I, in good conscience, cannot work for you anymore." I further indicated that his behavior did not only impact me; this mind-set could transfer into the manufacturing plant where many people of color were employed. It might even move into the community.

I knew from his facial expression that my comments meant my days were numbered.

Merry Christmas

The week after the incident with the VP of HR, a holiday party was scheduled at the corporate headquarters. The day arrived, and all fifty or so employees gathered in the conference room area. When I arrived, the party had already started; people were mingling and enjoying food and drinks. I arrived late because I had been finishing up some last-minute paperwork before the Christmas break.

It was a company tradition to have a grab-bag exchange at the party; everyone picked a name out of a hat and then brought a gift for that person. Because I had arrived late, I was informed by several people that it was time for me to open my present. It felt a little strange that everyone was encouraging my prompt participation. Unsuspectingly, I chalked up the enthusiasm to the beverages being served.

Under the Christmas tree was a good-size box neatly wrapped in holiday paper; my name was on it. As I opened the box, the room was exceptionally quiet. It seemed as if everyone else knew what was in the box. I tore off the paper, opened the box, and stared at a large green watermelon.

The room erupted with laughter. I sat motionless. The Accounting manager had the nerve to shout, "That was the biggest watermelon I could find."

With that, I stood up and said, "Happy Holidays. Good Night." For me, the party was over.

This incident took place in December 1973. I had already engaged in discussions to work for Digital Equipment Corporation. In the first quarter of the following year, I tendered my resignation. Ironically, at the time of my resignation, I was informed that my timing was favorable because I was going to be downsized for some reasons that remain unexplained. My instincts had been correct. I had known my days were numbered. How do you reload and regenerate?

"Sir. Sir."

In 1978, I traveled to Port St. Lucie, Florida, with a group of managers from Digital Equipment Corporation to a five-star resort for a business conference. We spent all day conducting or attending meetings regarding business goals, plans, direction, and metrics. The weather was warm, the grass was incredibly green, and the lawns were meticulously manicured. The conference agenda noted that a dinner was planned at an off-site restaurant for after we had participated in an all-day meeting in an air-conditioned conference room. Like others, I imagine, I was eager to get a change of scenery.

I went to my room, showered, and dressed in what I believed would be appropriate dinner attire. I chose white linen slacks, a white dress shirt, a red-and-navy tie, and a navy blazer with brass buttons. After fully dressing and checking my appearance in the mirror, I walked down to the lobby and stepped outside to get some fresh air. Looking at my watch, I realized that I was fifteen minutes early. I decided to just enjoy the weather and to wait for the other managers to arrive.

Soon thereafter, a black limousine sedan pulled up to the entrance of the resort. I was not particularly paying attention, but several times, I could hear an elderly woman's voice with a Southern accent saying, "Sir. Sir." I noted that each time she repeated "Sir. Sir," the voice got louder and more agitated. I finally turned to see who the woman might be calling.

Much to my amazement, an older white woman was calling out to me. As I turned toward her, she blurted out that she had tried several times to get my attention. She wanted me to get her luggage out of the limousine and bring it to the reception desk so she could check in.

Internally, being faced with this situation, I had to decide how to handle it. Reluctantly, I walked over to her limousine, removed her two suitcases, and carried them to the reception desk. She was not far behind me. As we approached the desk, the receptionist said, "Good evening. Will the two of you be checking in?" She followed with, "May I have your name and the credit card that you will be using?"

You should have seen the look on the white woman's face; her mouth was wide open, and she was suddenly speechless! I figured it was time for me to take charge of this situation. Facing the receptionist, I said, while pointing to my new companion, "This woman will be checking in; I am already a guest of the resort." Then, turning toward the older woman, I could see she had a tip in her hand. Politely, but emphatically, I managed to explained to her that, while I did not work for the resort, I was happy to assist her.

Looking back, I should have asked the receptionist for a king-size bed, room service, and a Do-Not-Disturb sign. I once again wonder how I reloaded and regenerated.

October Availability

If I remember correctly, the year was 1982 or 1983. I was a single parent living with my son in New Bedford, Massachusetts. Our home was a stately Georgian colonial of ten rooms and five baths. Many people commented that it was the most impressive-looking home on Rockdale Avenue.

Whether I liked it or not, I had to engage in the annual chore of raking leaves before winter arrived. One crisp Saturday morning, I carried my coffee cup outside, dressed for the weather in a cap and sweatshirt. I had raked for about two hours and had amassed several piles of leaves that still needed to be bagged. As I started on the second phase of the project, I was summoned from the lawn to the curb by a woman beeping her car horn several times. Initially, I ignored her because she was not anyone I knew.

Finally, exasperated, she shouted out to me. Presumptuously, she inquired, "Do you have any openings? I have a home in Padanaram. My lawn is in desperate need of raking. I also have other yard work that needs doing."

I gathered my thoughts as this well-to do woman made her inquiry. I could have burst her bubble but thought better of it. It is what you do with these situations when you're faced with them that makes the difference, so I politely indicated that my appointment book was completely filled. She replied, "Oh, that's unfortunate. I would have paid you well." Seeing no change of heart on my part, she drove off completely oblivious to the true nature of our encounter. She never gave it a thought that I might be the person who owned this home.

Master of the House

Once again during the seven years when my son and I lived in the stately Georgian colonial in New Bedford, Massachusetts, I had to address a situation that I did not ask for. On Saturday, midday, after I dropped my son off at the bowling alley, I returned home to get some housework done before going back to pick him up. I was dressed appropriately for doing chores, which included vacuuming and washing floors.

The doorbell chimed; I stopped and walked down the hallway to answer the front door. Opening the door and peering through the screen door, I was greeted by a well-dress white man with a briefcase. I said, "Good morning. Can I help you?"

He asked, "Is the master of the house at home?"

I immediately thought it was strange that this man did not ask, "Is the owner of the house at home?" or "Are you the owner?" Evidently, he had already concluded from the way I was dressed and from my black face that he could not possibly be speaking to a decision maker. I believe he thought he was talking to hired help.

I said to the gentleman, "Yes, he is home."

He then said, "Can you go and get him?"

I said, "Yes, I'll be happy to get him."

I turned, leaving him waiting at the front door. I took a left into my dining room, walked through the kitchen, turned right, and proceeded down the front hallway until I again reached the front door. I could see that the gentleman had a look of frustration and impatience, as there was no one walking behind me. He raised his voice slightly and in a tone approaching indignation asked, "Did you tell the master of the house there was someone who wanted to speak with him?"

I replied, "I certainly did. You are now absolutely talking to the master of the house."

Several shades of red-faced shame blossomed immediately. Apologies followed. Without acknowledging either, I politely replied, "I have all the house insurance I need—probably more than I need."

Nice Car

Working for Digital Equipment Corporation for twenty of my forty corporate years was most rewarding. I had my ups and downs; I got tested and retested, sometimes without even knowing I was being scrutinized. I developed friendships with my peers and I sought out a mentor. I knew I needed a mentor who would give me both guidance and direction as well as accept some degree of responsibility for my career growth. Obtaining a mentor helped me achieve a good deal of personal success.

As I was progressing with job growth and increased responsibility, my salary remuneration generally followed suit. The salary growth afforded me the opportunity to consider investments and luxury purchases. I bought a bigger home and a luxury automobile when I moved from New Bedford to Marlboro, Massachusetts. In fact, I finally bought the car of my dreams.

I made a decision, probably the wrong decision for many reasons, to purchase a new $65,000 BMW. A few weeks after I purchased the car, I was sitting in the cafeteria in the mill at DEC with several of my friends who worked with me in Human Resources. From across the table, one friend expressed his congratulations to me for buying such a beautiful automobile. Mimicking a current ad campaign, I replied, "Thanks. It's the ultimate driving machine."

Out of the blue, one of my peers, whom I did not particularly know, yelled out, "Yeah, the drug business must be good!"

I was stunned and hurt deeply. Before I could respond, several of my good friends came to my aid and candidly notified the offender that his remark was highly inappropriate. Ironically, within weeks, my boss—a white man—purchased an identical automobile. I guess the drug business was good for him, too.

LEGACY

$\mathcal{T}$he dictionary states that a legacy is the effect that a person had on another person or persons while he or she was alive. I want to share with you what I hope will be my legacy. As a younger man, I had no thought of legacy, but now I hope that my journey has meaning to at least one person on this earth.

Unity Bracelet

Disasters, both natural and those of human origin, seem to befall us with regularity: terrorist acts, suicide bombings, war, famine, floods, mudslides, hurricanes, earthquakes, and tsunamis that impact humankind. We reach out as neighbors across state, country, and continental borders. Worldwide generosity has not been limited by class, race, ethnicity, or any other artificial barrier that so often disconnects people from one another.

I wanted to extend this goodwill, mutual respect, and generosity to times when the disaster is not immediate; therefore, I designed a unity awareness bracelet that reflects the oneness of humankind. The Unity Bracelet was created.

Whether we're black, white, red, yellow, or brown, it is a fact that we all cast the same color shadow. The bracelet is sky blue with five circles of color representing the five races of the world. The text "We All Cast The Same Color Shadow" is debossed along the circumference of the bracelet. Unfortunately, artificial barriers still separate us. I am African American, Native American, English, and Irish. Like many Americans, I am a blend of many races and cultures. People often speak of inclusiveness and then go about their daily lives in a way that does not display that inclusiveness. My wish is to foster an everyday mind-set in those who wear the Unity Bracelet that they will conduct themselves with goodwill and respectfulness in their daily encounters.

This mind-set must have taken hold, because even after seven years since the bracelet's inception, many people approach me and, extending their arms proudly, say, "Look, I'm still wearing my bracelet."

Project 50/50

When I think about the impact that Project 50/50 Summer Enrichment Program for high school students has made on their lives, I know that only one person is capable of describing its true value. That is my friend of twenty-seven years, Mr. Mike Fields, Executive Director of the French River Education Center.

When I was being considered to receive the Outstanding Alumnus Award from Widener University (formerly Pennsylvania Military College), Mike Fields was requested to submit a synopsis of the impact of Project 50/50 Summer Enrichment Program, which was my brainchild, to the university's Alumni Selection Committee. The following is the text that he submitted:

It is with a great deal of pleasure that I share with you my personal history with Cadet #271, a man I came to know more than 27 years ago. A man as a visionary and advocate for inclusion and for offering opportunity to the under-represented and the disadvantaged youth among us.

It was the Spring of 1981, working as a special projects administrator for Oxford Public Schools, that I first met Cadet #271 where he worked as a Group Human Resources Manager for Technical Marketing. The Oxford/Digital partnership gave theatre to the idea of incorporating technology into education.

Cadet #271 knew this and saw the data which served as the genesis for a growing frustration. He was aware of who was buying personal computers and who was not. He further saw an ever-widening gap between those who have and those that did not have. He further realized the populations and demographics of households were most conspicuous by their absence in the high-tech workplace, particularly people of color and females. He arranged a meeting with the Oxford/French River Education Center to share with us his vision of what he would like to see happen for young students and how he thought we could together accomplish and achieve some goals.

Cadet #271's vision was to develop a Summer Enrichment Program for 8th, 9th and 10th grade students from districts that were identified as technology poor. He chose the name Project 50/50 because his goal was to achieve 50% representation of females, people of color and economically disadvantaged students.

These students would have the opportunity to attend a six-week program each summer for three consecutive years at no cost to them, their families or their school districts. His greatest challenge would be to find a way to fund the program at the 100% level. He began by petitioning Digital for Corporate funding, developing technology-based curriculum with assistance of Digital employees, and providing training for the teaching staff.

It now begs the question, was the vision, technology intervention, and the program successful? During the program years of 1990–1993, more than 950 students attended Project 50/50. Not only were the students taught how to use a computer, but they also learned the history of the computer, the use of the computer in the workplace, and the prerequisite skills required to work in the high-tech industry.

In addition, they learned how to navigate an outdoor orienteering course using a map and a compass. The students learned how to apply for employment for summer jobs. In their third and final summer, the students would simulate working for a small company with a mock budget where they would incorporate the computer skills they learned the two previous summers.

Cadet #271 and his Digital peers spent 543 person hours in 1982 developing the three-year program curriculum that was unique, engaging and hands-on. The program cost for these eight years was in excess of $700,000, all of which he was able to secure from Digital's Contribution Committee who immediately saw the value of Project 50/50.

As we tracked the students through their high school years, one of the outcomes we expected was that our students enrolled in more math, science and technology courses than what was required for graduation. We contracted with research consultants at Harvard University to gather data on the impact of Project 50/50. We tested the students in the California Achievement Test and the Tennessee Self-Concept Test. The data was so powerful and conclusive that it was decided to submit and present Project 50/50 to United States Department of Education's Joint Dissemination Review Panel in Washington, DC. The review panel announced the program worthy of replication and [decided] to provide funding and to bring the program to 20 school districts. For this, Cadet #271 received a Presidential Citation from President Ronald Reagan at the White House Rose Garden ceremony in June 1986.

And finally, the Project 50/50 staff-trained teachers were able to return to their respective school districts and train their colleagues after each summer in the use of technology in education. The number of students who benefitted directly from this training through the years is incalculable. So entrenched in technology were these same teachers that many of them took the initiative to seek out federal funding to purchase computers for their own schools, and some went on to become their districts' first technology coordinators.

I do not see Cadet #271 as much anymore, but we talk on the telephone at least once a year. But I am reminded constantly of what he did, what he accomplished, and the impact he had on the lives of students and teachers here and elsewhere when I look at my copy of his Presidential Citation, which is framed on my wall in my office.

In summary, working with Cadet #271 on Project 50/50 was one of the highlights of my professional career. He is a quality person and an outstanding alumnus of Pennsylvania Military College. His legacy to the world is that he inspired many people and made a significant contribution to their lives. We should all strive to do the same. I, myself, Mike Fields, am a better person because of my friendship with Cadet #271.

It is my goal to provoke the thinking of the readers who have invested their time reading this book. As you create and map out your own template for your life's journey, you will no doubt influence and have major impact on friends, family members, and even total strangers. Many people pass through our lives temporarily. As we interact with them and develop friendships through chance meetings or just brief conversations, we may enrich each other's lives and even become messengers in each other's circles of life.

Finally, it will always be my passion to inspire people, regardless of race, color, ethnic background, gender, religion, or sexual orientation, to look inside themselves and consider sharing their own stories. We all have one. I hope this book will serve as a catalyst for you to share your story.

Susan F. Barksdale
Robert D. Cody
Co-Chairmen
Board of Education

Irene Cornish
Superintendent of Schools

Stratford Board of Education

1000 East Broadway • Stratford, Connecticut 06615 • Phone (203) 385-4210 • Fax (203) 381-2012

March 17, 2009

Mr Louis Horner
c/o Widener University Alumni Engagement
One University Place
Chester, PA 19013

Dear Mr Horner

I would like to extend my congratulations to you for receiving the Widener University 2009 Alumni Award. According to a news account, you at one time lived in Stratford, CT and played Little League baseball here.

Your many contributions are a tribute to you and your family and for all that you have accomplished in your lifetime. You are an inspiration to the youth of today.

I congratulate and commend you on this most prestigious award.

Sincerely,

Irene Cornish
Superintendent

"Tantum eruditi sunt liberi" - Only The Educated Are Free

The Jackie Robinson Foundation

March 23, 2009

Ms. Meghan Radosh
Associate Director
Widener University Alumni Engagement
One University Place
Chester, PA 19013

Dear Friends,

Please accept my warmest greetings and congratulations as you gather to celebrate outstanding alumni on April 4, 2009. I am pleased to have the opportunity to recognize the many wonderful and hard fought achievements of Louis Horner. Like Number 42 Jackie Robinson, Louis was not only a great athlete, but is an exemplary representative of the unyielding pursuit of excellence in every aspect of his life; a pioneer for social justice and a successful business executive.

On this special occasion, you pay tribute to a distinguished individual who advances Jackie Robinson's bold vision of a brighter tomorrow for all humankind, and I join in congratulating Louis F. Horner for keeping the dream of progress alive.

Sincerely,

Jerry Lewis
Past President
The Jackie Robinson Foundation.

One Hudson Square • 75 Varick Street • 2nd Floor • New York, NY 10013-1917 • 212.290.8600 • fax 212.290.8081
550 South Hope Street • Suite 2300 • Los Angeles, CA 90071 • 213.330.7726 • fax 213.330.7701 • www.jackierobinson.org

PART THREE

One night, in the quiet of my thoughts, while neither fully awake nor asleep, I begin to think of what the future may hold. Imagining the events that will complete my time with my brothers of the Corps, I try to drift off.

THE FINAL REUNION

*T*he month of October jump-starts many events and celebrations, such as the World Series, college football, and, of course, college reunions.

College reunions had for many years been events to which the men of the Class of 1962 could journey to join in celebration and to renew friendships that have developed over the years, but there was something very different and very special about the next anticipated reunion of the Class of 1962. This event would be so special because it would be the last reunion and final tribute to the Band of Brothers.

Over the years, the number of brothers, both cadet and civilian, who participated in homecoming and marched on the field had dwindled to one. The image of only one cadet marching onto the football field at half time while carrying the flag standard of the Class of 1962 conjures in me wonderful memories of the past and reminds me of how much all of my brothers are missed.

It had been unanimously agreed that planning for five-year reunions no longer met the needs of the Class of 1962. We decided that the gatherings should appropriately take place every twelve to eighteen months, based on our ability to attend. It has been one year since our annual reunion. All the aforementioned events are about to take place once again: World Series, college football rivalries, and new class reunions.

As the last living survivor of the Class of 1962, whose responsibility was to continue to march on the field at homecoming, I decided to wait no longer. I would plan the last reunion and final tribute. It was the month of October, and I reminded my wife that I needed to make all the necessary preparations for the anticipated event: booking the hotel, hiring the DJ, and selecting the dinner menu for the 265 men of the Class of 1962. My wife was somewhat startled by my intense excitement. She asked inquisitively why I wanted to plan a full-fledged reunion when I was the last surviving brother of the Class of 1962. I immediately replied in a caring and forceful manner, "That is precisely why."

Through much effort on the part of my wife and me, all the preparations were completed. The trip to Ocean City, Maryland, was not long in miles, but nevertheless, it seemed tremendously long and was full of emotion. Many times since 2002, I had made this trip with anticipation of renewing friendships with new attendees and strengthening the bonds with the brothers who had somehow found it important to attend and participate in all the preceding reunions. This entire trip was full of introspection, reliving events and friendships past and present, while knowing all too well that this would be the final journey. Since I had recently been diagnosed with terminal cancer, at best, I would experience one more homecoming, one more change of season, and of course, the beauty of one more flock of geese flying south in a V formation. My wife and I arrived in Ocean City, Maryland, and checked in at Dunes Manor in the early afternoon.

Before going to our room, I checked with the concierge to make sure all the activities and events were set. We retired to our room for some much-needed rest and relaxation before making a final journey up to the hospitality suite, which was the beginning of three days of events and celebration. As the evening approached, my wife and I showered and dressed, then took the elevator up to the hospitality suite.

We entered the hospitality suite to a familiar venue of a table full of hors d'oeuvres, a keg of beer, a delivery of pizza, and several bottles of wine. On the table, standing up, was a yearbook of the Class of 1962. For the final time, I opened the yearbook and turned the pages one by one. As anticipated, an American flag was next to the bios of all the cadets except my own. That meant 264 flags and 264 salutes over the past sixty or seventy years. It now must be determined who will place the last American flag on my photo and issue a salute. I could think of only one person who could fulfill this need: my wife.

Laid out on a long banquet table with a white starched linen cloth was an array of uniforms that had become became the cadets' identity: fatigues, gray shirt and black tie, gray baseball jacket, overcoat, and, finally, a dress uniform complete with dress hat and plume. Laid across the dress uniform was a highly polished saber, the most beautiful picture you would ever want to see.

After a few glasses of beer and several glasses of wine, and hors d'oeuvres and pizza, my wife and I decided to call it a night and conclude day one.

The next day was a bright, sunny, brisk, fall day with an ocean breeze. My wife and I were awakened by the crashing waves of the ocean. We showered and dressed and made our way down to the breakfast buffet. The buffet consisted of cereals, fruits, pastries, waffles, bacon, ham, eggs, juice, and coffee. My wife and I filled our plates and scanned the room for a place to sit. The room was filled with unfamiliar faces, not the faces of the men of the Class of 1962. Although my wife and I could sense and feel the presence of the Band of Brothers, the breakfast conversation was more about each other rather than about past reunions.

After breakfast, a long walk down the boardwalk to take in some shopping and to burn off some calories from such a wonderful breakfast was welcomed. By the time we had walked to the end of the boardwalk, it was approaching the lunch hour. We decided on a light lunch of a seafood dish in anticipation of taking advantage of one of the many great restaurants where we had in the past shared many dinners with my classmates. When returning to the hotel after a full day on the boardwalk, we selected the restaurant, made a dinner reservation, showered, dressed, and then proceeded to the restaurant.

Once again, the ambience of the restaurant, the selection of food, dessert, and service was as it had been for so many preceding reunions. We were seated in an area of the restaurant that was sparsely populated and void of the men of the Class of 1962, their great jokes of military service and family memories. This dinner was a little bit different from breakfast, as my wife and I began again to talk about memories of each other but also began to open up and talk about former classmates and previous reunions.

It was as though the petals of a flower were beginning to open up ever so slightly. Being mindful and respectful of the past was appropriate and needed. Dinner lasted a couple of hours, and then my wife and I returned to Dunes Manor and retired for the night, concluding day two.

Day three, in terms of weather, was pretty much a carbon copy of days one and two: bright and sunny, with fresh ocean breeze. Waves broke softly where the ocean met the beach. Wanting to take advantage of the beautiful autumn weather, we had planned a full day, including a trip to Berlin, the antique capital of Maryland.

My wife and I took a leisurely walk in and out of antique shops and stopped in at a quaint hotel for lunch. This quaint hotel is famous for being the backdrop for the movie *Runaway Bride*. The entire town of Berlin is made up of quaint shops, antique stores, specialty restaurants, and restored buildings, but the pride and joy of Berlin is the wonderful and friendly residents. A trip to Berlin, Maryland, is not to be missed and had been thoroughly enjoyed by the Class of 1962 over the past fifty or sixty years. Berlin rated as the number-one sightseeing event.

As the day began to get away from us, my wife and I decided it was time to return to our hotel to experience one final tea time. A little rest and relaxation on Dunes Manor's deck, while watching the sunset concluded the daylight activities. Dinner, the final event, was yet to come.

At seven that evening, after showering and getting dressed for dinner, my wife and I proceeded downstairs to the dining room. All preparations had been carefully planned and executed. Care was given to every detail of this final dinner, the final tribute.

THE FINAL TRIBUTE

*M*y wife and I entered the dining room, which was decorated just as it had been for every other reunion. Our most immediate observation was of a sea of tables covered in white starched tablecloths with red overlays. The fine china place settings, incredible shiny crystal glasses, and sparkling silverware brightened the room. The place settings were 264 in number, representing each brother of the Class of 1962 who had been called home by God, with an American flag neatly draped over each chair.

As the last surviving cadet of the Class of 1962, I took my Pennsylvania Military College stein, which had been preserved all these years, and placed it on the dais. Since 1962, my brothers had all brought their steins to the reunion and placed them on the dais as a way of communicating that all were present and accounted for. As the years passed, the full complement of 265 steins visibly began to dwindle, and now, a nearly empty dais reflected the lone Pennsylvania Military College stein. Such a dichotomy. I proffered a crisp salute and returned to sit at the dining table with my wife. Sitting comfortably in her chair, my wife has tears noticeably streaming down her face. Her tears were confirmation that she knew all too well the pain I was feeling for the loss of my Band of Brothers. And she also knows all too well that very soon, she will feel the same pain of losing her husband to terminal cancer.

The dinner began as a waiter took our order for cocktails and appetizers. My wife and I waited for our orders and exchanged personal thoughts about how wonderfully the room was decorated, with the sea of red, white, and blue American flags draped over the empty chairs. Although the tables and chairs were noticeably empty, my wife and I again felt that 264 spirits of the Pennsylvania Military College, Class of 1962, and I, the surviving cadet of the Band of Brothers, were all together again for a final reunion and final tribute.

The waiter returned with the drinks and appetizers. Shortly, the dinner would follow. While leisurely enjoying our meal, once again, our conversation turned to previous reunions. I began to reminisce about my four years of college and the origin of the Band of Brothers. Sustained emotion and flowing tears helped mark the final tribute to the Pennsylvania Military College Class of 1962.

The night went quickly, and it was time to perform the final tribute. As the last surviving cadet of the Band of Brothers, I turned toward my wife of forty-plus years and gently touched her like I had never touched her before. This touch seemed to tell her that this event would never be replicated. I rose from my chair slowly and made my way to the dais, where the sole Pennsylvania Military College stein rested all alone. After clutching my stein as if it were valuable crystal, I raised my arm straight up toward the ceiling of the dining room.

In a most caring and tender way, and yet with the strength of a drum major with his baton, I gave praise to God, country, the university, and the men of the Class of 1962. I continued the final tribute by saying tenderly, "God, this is the final reunion and my final tribute to the Band of Brothers. I ask only one final question of you before I myself am called home and cross over the bar. Will you please tell me, who will water the flowers?"

With that, I saluted, performed an about-face, and walked slowly back to our table to be greeted by my tearful wife. With outstretched arms, she embraced me with a tender kiss as if we both had shared the reading of lessons from geese. There was a moment of silence, and she leaned over and whispered to me, "My darling, my love, the men of the Class of 1962 will always be known as the Band of Brothers and will all march again together in heaven."

And with that, day three had come to its final curtain.

PASS IN REVIEW

The final reunion for the Class of 1962, the Band of Brothers, in Ocean City, Maryland, had finally concluded, with empty chairs and empty tables. The empty tables with the white tablecloths, and red overlays and incredible shiny crystal glasses will continue to glisten in the mind of the last surviving cadet and his wonderful wife. What we see with our eyes can sometime cloud our vision, but what we feel in our hearts can never be compromised until the final beat of our hearts.

Now it was time to make the final trip to homecoming weekend in Chester, Pennsylvania, at Widener University. This trip represented the final gathering, the final march, and, of course, the final salute that I had the privilege of conducting.

I now had the painstaking responsibility as the last surviving cadet to take down the banner that read, "Welcome Class of 1962." My wife and I would gently and meticulously fold this banner for the final time. The banner might possibly find its final resting place in the Pennsylvania Military College Museum on the campus of Widener University. Our sons, daughters, grandchildren, and other family members in succeeding years will be able to observe and cherish a piece of the PMC history.

My wife and I packed and checked out of Dunes Manor Hotel for the final time. Many of the staff over the years have become like family as they made the gathering of the Band of Brothers what we could call a home away from home.

The bright, sunny, crisp October air and the sea breeze of Ocean City, Maryland, became a faded memory as we covered the miles and Chester, Pennsylvania, came closer. The trip took on a most unusual atmosphere; my wife and I were unusually quiet. We were consumed by our thoughts about individual and collective experiences spanning the past seventy to eighty years. Memories of bonding, friendships, and the love and deaths of 264 of your brothers can become all-consuming.

Finally, the highway sign on the New Jersey Turnpike indicating that we were entering Chester, Pennsylvania, home of Widener University, appeared. It came as a shock and a welcome surprise to my wife and me that this final trip, driven many times, for some inexplicable reason seemed to be shorter. I can only conclude that the mind has a way of consuming you and of giving comfort in the time of need.

As my wife and I approached the Widener University campus, we looked up and then at each other for confirmation of what we both had just seen. Draped across the road, tied high on the telephone poles, was a huge red, white, and yellow banner that glistened with the words "Welcome Class of 1962." This was the final raising of this banner, and it might also find its proper resting place side by side with our treasured banner.

The campus today was very crowded with alumni, and we could feel the excitement in the air of homecoming weekend.

The first order of business is finding the alumni reception building to register and check in. After locating the building and checking in, it was off to find the tents where the alumni cookout with wine and beer would take place. For some strange reason, the crowd of alumni, guests, and students participating in the various activities and events was usually large. If I had to guess, I would estimate that the crowd, in the range of twenty thousand people, would fill the stadium for the annual homecoming football game.

After eating lunch and participating in some much-anticipated libations, my wife and I made our way to our assigned seats in the stadium shortly before the start of the football game. With the start of the game, all kinds of emotions began to make their final visit to my heart. I was flooded with thoughts of the final game, the final luncheon, the final half-time celebration, the final gathering of one cadet, and, more importantly, the final salute from the Class of 1962, the Band of Brothers.

As the end of the second quarter approached, the score indicated that the football game was going well for the home team, the Widener University Pride. It was time for me, the last surviving cadet of the Class of 1962, to get up and make my way to the end zone to take my place behind three alumni classes who would march on the field before me. I kissed my wife and embraced her with a hug that made her feel as though all 265 men of the Band of Brothers were embracing her.

The second quarter ended, and the final time for the pass and review by the Band of Brothers was about to begin. The music began, and the first group of alumni from a preceding classes stepped off as though they had never lost the step or rhythm required by marching cadets. The stadium announcer identified each of the preceding alumni classes. Now, at last, the final time had come to march off with the Class of 1962 flag blowing straight out into the crisp air of October. I, as the surviving cadet, hesitated for a moment, which seemed like a lifetime, to gain an unusual amount of separation between myself and the previous alumni classes.

The final march, the final salute, and the final gathering of the Band of Brothers commenced. It was now obvious and apparent to everyone that there was something strange, emotional, spiritual, and special about a lone cadet approaching almost one hundred years old could harness the energy and stature of a cadet representing the Class of 1962. As I marched straight ahead, the Class of 1962 flag could be said to be flying as it had never flown before, giving credence to the final march. The stadium announcer identified the lone cadet and the Class of 1962, and then the marching music that had accompanied the halftime festivities stopped.

The stadium of twenty thousand alumni, guests, and students went silent. At this point, I gave a glance to my left, where my wife was standing with tears rolling down her cheeks. I acknowledged her loving presence and her continued love and caring since we met so long ago. As the last surviving cadet, I returned to looking straight ahead to continue my final march and to give my final salute from the Class of 1962, the Band of Brothers. When I reached the fifty-yard line, the silence continued. As the last cadet, I raised the Class of 1962 flag to give the fitting and final salute for all 264 of my brothers. As the flag reached its maximum salute height, a stream of air came just above the flag. At this moment, I heard a voice that encouraged me to look up; to my surprise, high up in the sky appeared several flocks of geese—265 of them—flying in a V formation. Tears began to stream down my face. Finally, with my heart beating intensely, like that of a drum major, something or someone tugged at my heart to look behind me. The stadium crowd all felt this sudden stream of air, and although they could not been seen by anyone except me, the lone cadet, the spirits of 264 of my brothers, the Class of 1962, were marching with me.

As the bagpiper played, I gave the final salute. I lifted my head and eyes to the heavens and whispered, "I now know who will water the flowers." You answered my prayer, God; it is you.

Finally, in 2035, as the season changed from winter to spring, the memories of the final reunion faded, the last bed of red, white, and blue perennial flowers had been planted. Each spring, the flowers will face the sun and blossom, forming once again a red, white, and blue American flag at the base of a white marble stone.

Thereafter, on every graduation day a slight shower of rain, that some might say are tears from heaven, sustains life and provides an annual salute to the Class of 1962, the Band of Brothers.

Pennsylvania Military College

We, the members of the Corps of Cadets,
dedicate this site to PMC and those
classmates who are gone, but never
forgotten.

THE THEME

*F*or the theme of our class, Cadet #383 suggested we borrow from the lyrics from Tom Hanks's TV series *Band of Brothers*, in which songwriter Frank Musker used the following lyrics:

Requiem for a Soldier
You never lived to see what you gave to me
A shining dream of hope and love, life and liberty
With a host of brave unknown soldiers from your company
You will live forever in our memory
In the field of sacrifice heroes paid the price
Young men who died for old men's war
Gone to paradise
We are all one big band of brothers
And one day you'll see we can live together
When all the world is free I wish you'd lived to see
All you gave to me
Your shining dream of hope
And love, life, and liberty
We are all one great band of brothers
And one day you'll see we can live together when all the world is
free

Offered by Cadet #383, William Muehsam

THE FINAL SALUTE

As a tribute to the love, respect, and camaraderie of my brothers, the men of Pennsylvania Military College Class of 1962 who are no longer with us to continue the march to the drummer, I offer these words from "Crossing the Bar" by Alfred Tennyson.

Twilight and evening bell,
And after that the dark!
And may there be no sadness of farewell,
When I embark;

For tho' from out our bourne of Time and Place
The flood may bear me far,
I hope to see my Pilot face to face
When I have crost the bar.

THE FINAL MARCH

THE CLASS OF 1962
BROTHERS WHO HAVE CROSSED THE BAR

John Henry Alexander
George Francis Bennett
Kenneth Edward Blanchard Jr.
Harry L. Boyce
Barry John Case
Frank Joseph Colantuno
C. David Cole
William Alexander Diament
Louis William Dicave Jr.
Joseph Albert DiEduardo
John Robert Dinardo
George Leonard Fossett Jr.
Richard Creighton Gilmour
William Graner
William Gruzinski
Bruce Martin Hanley
George Albert Horn
Barry Kalinsky
Barry Richard Keith
Lawrence Bruce Krumanocker
Peter H. Lake
Peter John Larkin
Patrick Leno
Daniel Francis Monahan
Robert Chandler Moore
William Ernest Muehsam
Frank William Odiotti
Gary Michael Piff
Franklyn E. Rideout
Richard Henry Robey
Robert Gail Saunders
Ralph William Seitz Jr.

Arthur E. Scortese
Joseph Michael Spadafina
Edward Albert Steimetz
James Haskell Stevenson
Paul Jay Sykes
John Michael Tysall
(Compilation as of October 31, 2015)

CIVILIAN BROTHERS WHO HAVE CROSSED THE BAR
Richard Adam
Frederick Clement Faust
Donald Charles Fehr
John F. Glatts
Thomas Hickey
John A. Hoffman
William Kelly
Donald James Konegan
Barry B. Latham
John Jay Leatherman
Thomas Nolan
James Gentry Perry
William Spangler Sellers
Gerald Cliff Willis
(Compilation as of October 31, 2015)

Above the Clouds

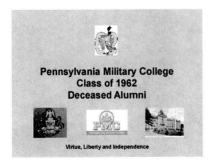

**Pennsylvania Military College
Class of 1962
Deceased Alumni**

Virtue, Liberty and Independence

John Alexander

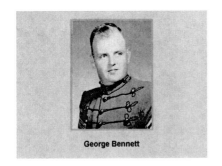

George Bennett

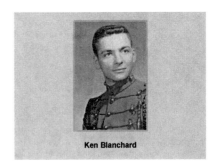

Ken Blanchard

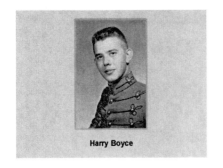

Harry Boyce

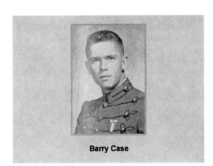

Barry Case

Frank Colantuno

Dave Cole

Alex Diament

Lou DiCave

Joe DiEduardo

John Dinardo

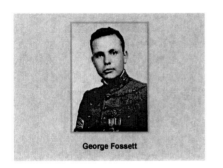

George Fossett

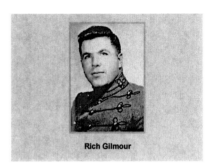

Rich Gilmour

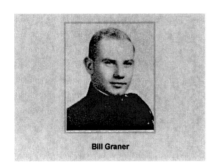

Bill Graner

Bill Gruzenski

Bruce Hanley

George Horn

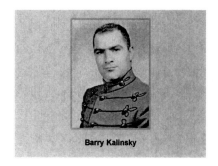

Barry Kalinsky

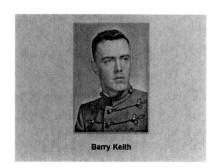

Barry Keith

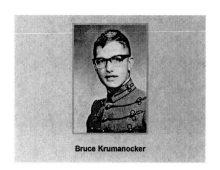

Bruce Krumanocker

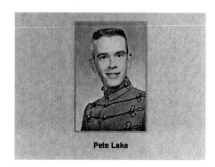

Pete Lake

Pete Larkin

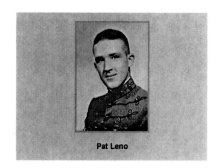

Pat Leno

Dan Monahan

Bob Moore

Bill Muehsam

Frank Odiotti

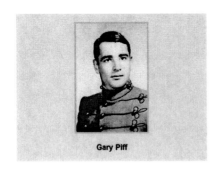

Gary Piff

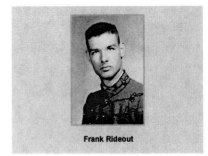

Frank Rideout

Richard Robey

Bob Saunders

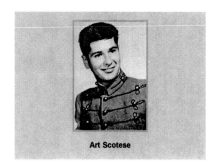

Art Scotese

Bill Seitz

Joe Spadafina

Ed Steinmetz

Jim Stevenson

Paul Sykes

Richard Adam

Fred Faust

Donald Fehr

Jack Glatts

Tom Hickey

John Hoffman

Don Konegan

William Kelly

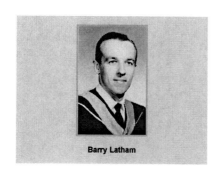

Barry Latham

John Leatherman

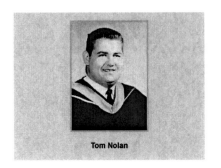

Tom Nolan

Jim Perry

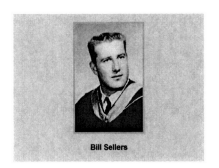

Bill Sellers

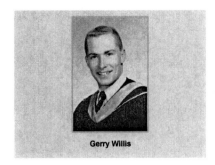

Gerry Willis

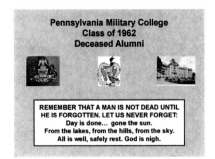

**Pennsylvania Military College
Class of 1962
Deceased Alumni**

REMEMBER THAT A MAN IS NOT DEAD UNTIL
HE IS FORGOTTEN. LET US NEVER FORGET:
Day is done… gone the sun.
From the lakes, from the hills, from the sky.
All is well, safely rest. God is nigh.

PARALLEL STONES

I look about and see a field of stones
For men and women from far and near
Laid to rest as human flesh and bones
In silent rows of markers to be held dear.

They are of the military that needs no tears.
Like other comrades, all have given their best.
Over centuries of sacrifice. they have no fears.
For a simple reward of cloth upon their chest.

They've heard the roar of the engines from above
And the fire of canon upon the sea.
They have given us freedoms that we love
With the ultimate for all who have been free.

Good or bad for you are allowed to say,
But amongst the stones a silent bow is met
For what we do and all we have today.
Today thank a vet.

Offered by Cadet #396, Donald Zero

ROLL CALL

And now this journey, which each of you has chosen to take with me, has reached its destination. I leave you this final message.

All cadets are present and accounted for. We, the Class of 1962, the Band of Brothers, are assembled and ready to take our final march together with you.

* * *

Awakening during the night,
my thoughts drift once again to future events.

EPILOGUE

Several hours, through both lunch and dinner, passed before I finished telling Michael Barton the story of the first half of my life. He had already finished the half of the manuscript that he had found on the train. Now he had the complete story and understood why I felt it must be shared with the world.

As our meeting came to a close, dusk approached. The setting sun's rays glistened off the fiberglass boats moored at the marina. Standing on the dock, we both looked up at the same time. A flock of geese were flying in V formation, heading south. Turning to face each other, we shook hands. I felt we had somehow made a connection intellectually, emotionally, and spiritually.

Michael had made a reservation at the Chatham Bars Inn so he could visit with a college classmate. He was driving back home to Stratford in the morning. As we said good-bye, I said to him, "Oh, one more thing." Then I reached in my pocket and pulled out a Unity Bracelet, which I handed to him.

His eyes welled up with tears, and he said, "Thank you so much. I now have everything I need to move forward with my task of bringing this story to film someday. We will, I am sure, meet again."

* * *

Michael and Cadet #271 kept in contact for several more years; their friendship grew through both correspondence and face-to-face visits. One sunny afternoon, Michael received a telephone call from his wife. She had just learned that Cadet #271 had died.

Michael imagined his friend in full military regalia marching toward heaven. He attended the funeral, which concluded with a military gun salute. It was now time for him to make good on his promise to bring Cadet #271's story to film.

ACKNOWLEDGMENTS

*T*here are many people who, like myself, are reminded every day of their race, color, ethnicity, gender, or sexual orientation. I believe it is imperative that we reject judgments based on these factors. Life is a gift that should not be minimized by those who wish to categorize us.

If today I were called to arms to defend freedom, I would want to go into battle with my classmates, the cadets of Peekskill Military Academy Class of 1958 and the men of Pennsylvania Military College Class of 1962. These men and my close friends from Stratford High School would the people who would welcome me home or, in the event of my death, honor my service.

There are those whose friendship and support have graced my life. With gratitude, I acknowledge Linda Stewart, Dorothea Maynard, Russell Maynard, Carmella Matarazzo Fawver, Daniel Del Vecchio, Keith Bodden, Ron Romanwicz, Rochelle Bilz, Robert Hawley, Karen Louda, Chuck Nuese, Debra Sansone, Laura Shabott, Joseph Beraducci, and Elizabeth Beraducci. Each of these friends offered continuing support, read rough drafts, and offered feedback toward revision. Some acted as my editors and worked tirelessly while sacrificing their own personal time. Thank you all.

Louis Franklin Horner

ABOUT THE AUTHOR, CADET #271

*I*n 1951, Louis Horner was the first African American to participate in Little League Baseball in Stratford, Connecticut; in 1955–1956, the first African American class president at his school; in 1957–1958, the first African American accepted in and to graduate from the now defunct Peekskill Military Academy in Peekskill, New York; and from 1958 to 1962, the first African American to play varsity baseball and varsity basketball at Pennsylvania Military College (now Widener University) in Chester, Pennsylvania, which he graduated from in 1962 with a degree and a commission as a second lieutenant in the United States Army Signal Corps.

Louis Horner, as a human resource manager with Digital Equipment Corporation, was a contributing force behind one of the nation's most successful inner-city manufacturing plants in Springfield, Massachusetts. Louis Horner received a Presidential Citation from President Ronald Reagan in 1985 for designing a computer enrichment program that served as a model for several thousand children nationwide.

Mr. Horner considers his meeting Jackie Robinson at Ebberts Field a significant event that gave him a person to look up to. For the author, as for any others who have experienced the bitter taste of racial, ethnic, or religious bias, the journey continues. He decided to write this book about the Pennsylvania Military College class of 1962.

In 2008, Paul Gauvin, writer for the *Barnstable Patriot*, Hyannis, Massachusetts, wrote that Barack Obama was on the cusp of becoming the first African American president of the United States. In 1947, Jackie Robinson was the first African American Major League Baseball player. Carl Stokes of Cleveland was the first elected African American mayor of a major city. In 2001, General Colin Powell became the first African American Secretary of State.

He wrote that Louis F. Horner was in the vanguard of the army that hurdled racial barriers. The article stated that Horner should be added to the list of pioneers first to penetrate the color barrier in their own environments and to parlay that penetration into significant services to humankind.

In April 2009, the author was selected as the Outstanding Alumnus of the Year by Widener University. Later honoring Mr. Horner for his accomplishments, he was invited him to throw out the first pitch of the alumni baseball game during Homecoming Weekend in 2011. The vote had already been taken; Louis was participating.

Appendix A

The History of PMC, 1821–1972

Offered by Loretta Shaffer wife of Cadet #363

Pennsylvania Military College was the second oldest military college in the United States, preceded only by the United States Military Academy at West Point.

1821 THE BULLOCK SCHOOL was established by John Bullock, a Quaker pacifist, in Wilmington, Delaware. The school was known for academic achievement and character building. Samuel Alsop, a mathematician and scholar from Philadelphia, Pennsylvania, taught at the school and, upon the death of John Bullock in 1847, assumed administration of the school.

1839 WILMINGTON LITERARY INSTITUTE was established by Reverend Corry Chambers, an Episcopal priest.

1847 WILMINGTON LITERARY SCIENTIFIC AND MILITARY INSTITUTE was founded by Reverend Corry Chambers and Alden Partridge, a West Point graduate, professor, and acting superintendent.

1853 THE HYATT SELECT SCHOOL FOR BOYS was established by Theodore Hyatt when he combined the Wilmington Presbyterian Church Schools with the former Bullock School, which he purchased from Samuel Alsop.

1858 WILMINGTON LITERARY SCIENTIFIC AND MILITARY INSTITUTE failed, and the **HYATT SELECT SCHOOL FOR BOYS** was incorporated under the charter of the failed school.

1859 Theodore Hyatt changed the name of **HYATT SELECT SCHOOL FOR BOYS** to **DELAWARE ACADEMY**. Additionally, Delaware governor William Burton ordered certain public arms delivered to the military academy. Until that time, the cadets had been marching with brooms. Theodore Hyatt became a colonel as an aide de camp to the governor. The student body grew from fifty to eighty-three.

1855–1859 Theodore Hyatt was president of the school, with a board of directors that included Reverend Corry Chambers.

1860 Delaware had torn loyalties between the North and the South. An organized military company attempted to have the governor turn over arms from the academy to them. The governor refused. A Southern sympathizer stole the arms from the school.

1862 Because of pressures in Delaware, Colonel Hyatt sought to move the school to Pennsylvania and arranged a lease for property in West Chester. The school received a charter from the state of Pennsylvania as a primary school and college to last into perpetuity. The board of trustees was concerned that the school's name had local and limited connotations and petitioned the court to change the name to **PENN-SYLVANIA MILITARY ACADEMY**. Pennsylvania provided a full compliment of arms to the school.

1865 The lease on the West Chester property expired and the land had to be sold by the heirs of the owner. Colonel Hyatt did not want to purchase it and sought another site.

1865 The academy used the Chester Crozer Normal School facility in Uplandboro, which had served as a military hospital during the war.

1866 A baseball team was started at the academy.

1867 Upon Chester Crozer's death in 1867, the family gave the property to the Baptist Church and the academy once again had to relocate. A group of citizens in Chester formed a company, applied for a corporate charter, purchased property, and erected buildings for a permanent home for Pennsylvania Military Academy. The corporation registered as the Military Academy Stock Company, issued stock, and purchased twenty acres between Morton Avenue and Sixteenth Street and Chesnut Street and Melrose Avenue at $1000 per acre. The construction contract was awarded to John Sheduck and Sons for $38,875. The architect was John Crump.

1868 Dedication of the building **Old Main** took place. Tuition to the academy was five hundred dollars per semester.

1869 The Army assigned Captain Thomas J. Lloyd to the academy.

1869–1870 A wing of additional classrooms and a lab were added to the main building.

1871 The Army established a US detail system at the academy and appointed Major Francis H. Bates.

1879 A football team was started at the academy.

1882 Fire struck the main building; cadets were sent home for three weeks and after returned to classes held at the Ridley Park Hotel. **Old Main** was rebuilt and opened in September.

1886 Electric lights came to **Old Main**.

1887 Colonel Theodore Hyatt died.

1891 **Colonel Theodore Hyatt Observatory** was built with donations from alumni.

1892 Typhoid fever killed five cadets. The school was closed temporarily. On December 12, a petition was made to the Court of Common Pleas to amend the charter and change the name of the school to **PENNSYLVANIA MILITARY COLLEGE**.

1898 About seventy graduates served in the Spanish American War, with ranks from private to brigadier general.

1899–1902 John Wanamaker served as president of the board of trustees.

1903 The War Department began to list the most distinguished military institutions based on annual inspections. **PENNSYLVANIA MILITARY COLLEGE** was ranked in the top ten from 1903–1914.

1904 The college's athletic board was formed of faculty and students to take responsibility for baseball, football, hockey, and gymnastics.

1905 Basketball was introduced to **PMC**.

1914 The War Department established a new classification for military institutions. **PMC** was considered a college rather than an institution because of the number of enrollments. Although no longer ranked, the college remained strong and maintained a favorable reputation within the military.

1907–1915 Enrollment at the college declined.

1916 The National Defense Act established ROTC. Low enrollment prevented **PMC** from applying for a unit. World War I caused a deferral of ROTC nationwide until the war ended. Frank Hyatt, son of Charles Hyatt, became treasurer of the college, expanded the curriculum, and established **PENNSYLVANIA MILITARY PREP SCHOOL** to increase the enrollment of the college.

1917 An existing building (**Hyatt Hall**) was purchased, as well as an additional five acres so a gymnasium and a pool could be built. Funding was solicited from alumni.

1919 Charles E. Hyatt Armory was opened. **PMC** remained a private college, owned and controlled by the Hyatt family. It was a for-profit college and not entitled to tax relief.

1926–1927 The construction of **Memorial Stadium** took place behind **Old Main**.

1930 Charles E. Hyatt died; Frank Kelso Hyatt became president.

1932 Enrollment again began to decline, due in some part to the Depression, increased tuition costs, lack of accreditation, and lack of receipt of federal funds because of the school's for-profit, privately owned status.

1934 The board of trustees searched for a way to change the ownership of the college to benefit from federal tax relief. The college financial statement showed an indebtedness of $365,000.

1935 Additional losses of $31,000 were reported.

1936 When a bank called in a loan for $117,000, the college filed for bankruptcy. The court allowed the college to remain open under court order. Military Academy Stock Company sold its stock to the Hyatt Foundation. The federal government recognized the foundation as not for profit, but local officials did not grant it the same status.

1942 Enrollment grew from 153 cadets in 1936 to 281 cadets. **Loveland Victory Hall** and **Webb Hall** were purchased to accommodate the increase of cadets.

1943 Enrollment dropped to seventy cadets when the Enlisted Reserve Corps went on active duty. The college accepted an Army Specialized Training Unit of 300 men.

1943–1946 Additional Army students enrolled and the college was able to sustain itself financially. The college was reorganized under the Federal Bankruptcy Law. Edwin Howell was considered the most important person responsible to the survival of **PMC** during the reorganization.

1945 Clarence R. Moll was appointed as registrar of the college and as prep school headmaster.

1946 The prep school was accredited for the first time in many years. Veterans were attending the college as civilian students and ended the era of **PMC** as an exclusive military college.

1947 By this time, the prep school had become a completely separate entity from the college. The First edition of the *Dome* was published. Clarence R. Moll was appointed to the newly established position of dean of admissions and student personnel.

1948 The polo team and the cavalry were dropped. Enrollment grew to 1002 cadets and civilian students.

1948–1952 Money was raised to build **THE MEMORIAL LIBRARY**, a necessary asset for the college to gain accreditation by the Middle Atlantic States Association.

1949 Veteran enrollment declined. The college began to accept day cadets.

1952 Frank Hyatt retired. Edwin Howell was appointed interim president. The drill team was inducted as Company Q, Fifth Regiment of the Pershing Rifles.

1953 The board of trustees appointed Major General Edward Elliott McMoreland as **president of PMCollege**. President Major General McMoreland appointed Clarence R. Moll in charge of preparation for accreditation. George Hansel was appointed the football coach.

1955 The prep school was discontinued.

1957 **PMC** was accredited by the Middle Atlantic States Association.

1953–1958 President Major General Mc Moreland was active in the local community and civic organizations, expanding the Day Student Program to include civilians and establishing the Pennsylvania Military College Evening Division. Clarence R. Moll was appointed as vice president of **PMC**.

1958 **Howell Hall** was dedicated. George Hansel was appointed athletic director. Frank Hyatt died.

1959 President Major General McMoreland retired. Clarence R. Moll was appointed president of **PMC**.

1962 The final class of day cadets graduated.

1965 Kirkbride Hall was dedicated.

1966 The college changed its name to **PENNSYLVANIA MILITARY COLLEGES** (PMC and Penn Morton College) and became coed with the addition of a nursing program.

1968–1972 The **PENNSYLVANIA MILITARY COLLEGES** experienced severe money problems related to construction and reduced enrollment. Cadet enrollment and retention were at low points. The future of the Corps of Cadets was studied.

May 20, 1972 The final assembly of the Corps of Cadets took place. The corps acted with dignity, embodying the words found on a plaque in **Old Main** that many view as what PMC was all about:

When wealth is lost, nothing is lost
When health is lost, something is lost
When honor is lost, all is lost

PMC colors were retired. The final sheathing of the Corps of Cadets' saber took place. At 4:03 p.m., the Corps of Cadets was dismissed.

Appendix B

Questionnaire

1) What prompted you to enroll in Pennsylvania Military College?

2) What significant events do you remember about Pennsylvania Military College?

3) How do you think you have changed as an individual during your four years at Pennsylvania Military College?

4) Are these changes different from those that occurred had you attended a nonmilitary college?

5) What unique factors at Pennsylvania Military College contributed to these changes?

6) How did your four years at Pennsylvania Military College have a specific influence on your life in the following areas?

7) Military career?

8) Professional life outside of the military?

9) Personal life and interpersonal relationships with family and friends?

10) What do you recall as your most pleasant memories and/or experiences at Pennsylvania Military College?

11) What did you learn from these?

12) What do you recall as your worst memories and/or experiences at Pennsylvania Military College?

13) What did you learn from these?

14) Did you ever contemplate transferring from Pennsylvania Military College to another school? Talk about the events that led up to these thoughts and your final decision to remain.

15) Overall, what learnings, beliefs, and life messages did you take with you after graduation?

16) Describe one friendship, from all that you formed, [that] made the greatest impression upon you at Pennsylvania Military College.

17) Looking back at your life, describe one friendship, from all that you formed, that has had the greatest impact on your adult life, either personally or professionally. This can be the same friendship or a different friendship than the one chosen from the previous question.

Neither of these questions supposes that you have had continued contact with your fellow cadet or cadets indicated.

18) What importance do reunions have for you? Why do you attend?

19) What do you see as the common threads that bind us, the men of the Class of 1962, that are unique to us and our time spent together?

CPSIA information can be obtained at www.ICGtesting.com
Printed in the USA
LVOW10s0510170216

475376LV00012B/31/P

9 781457 545054